Into the Ruins

Issue 5
Spring 2017

Published May 2017 by Figuration Press
Portland, Oregon

Into the Ruins is a project and publication of Figuration Press,
a small publication house focused on alternate visions of the future
and alternate ways of understanding the world,
particularly in ecological contexts.

intotheruins.com

figurationpress.com

ISBN 13: 978-0-9978656-3-9
ISBN 10: 0-9978656-3-6

Editor's Note:
It's amazing how much time one can spend tracking down specific rules pertaining to
suspension points, hyphenation, numerals versus words, and the finer points of
formatting lyrics quoted in dialogue. While I thank the gods for *The Chicago
Manual of Style*, I'm not sure I thank them for my pedantry.

Comments and feedback always welcome at editor@intotheruins.com
Comments for authors will be forwarded.

Issue 5
Spring 2017

TABLE OF CONTENTS

PREAMBLE

STORIES

REVIEWS

PREAMBLE

A Valley's Echo Through Time

by Joel Caris

In April, my fiancée and I packed our car and departed on a road trip for Joshua Tree National Park. Looking forward to warmth, aridity, and long hikes in the desert after an unusually eventful Pacific Northwest winter that showed little signs of ending, we headed east and then south, driving toward an eventual intersection in California with U.S. Route 395 in anticipation of a mountainous path down the eastern side of the state, skirting the Sierra Nevada mountain range. Of course, after this winter, a late season snow storm was hitting the mountains just as we left, so we bought a set of chains, crossed our fingers, and hoped for the best.

Our luck held enough that the snow proved a non-obstacle, providing little more than a consistent passing of beautiful snow-covered mountains and hills along the way—some places worse than others, yet all of them sporting clear roads and mostly dry pavement. Over the course of several days, we worked our way down through Klamath Falls, Oregon, around and past Lake Tahoe, and then over a series of high mountain passes between there and Bishop, California, with stops at multiple high mountain lakes in between. After this long trip through high elevation, we dropped back down toward the desert and, perhaps an hour outside of a morning departure from Bishop, found ourselves pulling into the Manzanar National Historic Site.

For those unaware, Manzanar was an internment camp where American citizens of Japanese descent and Japanese immigrants were incarcerated during World War II. Noting its location along our route while planning our trip, we had decided to stop off there during our final leg into Joshua Tree, and thus we arrived at the site on a Tuesday morning. Nestled in Owens Valley with the Sierra Nevadas looming high and imposing to the west and the Inyo Mountains sitting to the east, the desolate site struck an ominous note with its replica guard tower at the entrance and surrounding dry, ghosted land.

There are plenty of things I know far too little about, but probably the most consequential is history. It was a subject that largely bored me in school, though looking back now I recognize that as more about the way it was presented—in that usual dry way, focused on facts and figures, with narratives that hardly earned the name and ignored all the messy and fascinating complications of a history driven by humanity—than about my innate interest or lack thereof in the past affairs of humans. If anything, I now find history quite compelling, and am forever intrigued by the ways in which our forebears dealt with the triumphs and challenges of the past. It's just that I want those activities presented as human stories, replete with all their glorious imperfections, than as timelines of events divorced from their true meanings—and often misrepresented and mythified to boot.

As it happens, the visitor center and museum at Manzanar does a fine job of presenting the human stories of Manzanar specifically and the Japanese internment in general. It is a subject that I came into the visit knowing little about, which strikes me as something of an indictment both of myself and of our country's educational system. But then, "reflective" and "self-aware" are, sadly, not terms that I strongly identify with the United States; history—so I suppose, given American attitudes—is a superfluous subject with little relevance to a population forever and frantically searching for the next great innovations, the next cutting edge technologies, the perpetual progress that somehow seems to most always manifest in the (unacknowledged) rehashing of the same old tired tropes and stale beliefs. Obviously history has no bearing on such an important process, and certainly has nothing helpful or worthwhile to offer a society constantly moving forward, forward, forward. Or so it seems from our nation's common attitude. And yet, moving through Manzanar's visitor center and reading the stories of prisoners at the camp, I couldn't help but see the way our endless capacity for fear and cruelty echoes throughout history and, at the same time, marvel at the ways in which people come together to form community and help one another in daunting and destructive times.

Certain anecdotes from the histories stay with me: the volunteer who came early to the site to help build the camp, knowing that friends, family, and neighbors would be joining him soon enough and wanting to prepare their coming home for them with care; those who convinced themselves before coming to the camp that President Roosevelt's executive order was for their own safety and for the good of the country; the woman who spoke about how limited the work options were for Japanese Americans in California, and how the necessity to create a functioning economy within a camp of ten thousand people led to a variety of work that would have otherwise been off limits in broader society. These anecdotes blended with the harsh recreations of camp facilities: the straw-stuffed bags meant to serve as mattresses, the sparse and barren barracks, the rows of unseparated toilets and communal showering areas offering not even the hint of privacy. And weaving through all of this were stories of the internees' efforts to beautify their surroundings in whatever ways they could, from building elegant furniture out of rudimentary materials to crafting intricate carvings of birds to creating on-site gardens. The push and pull of the stories—the horror and cruelty, the caring and generosity, the craft and intent, and the sorrow echoing throughout the center as the immense failure of one country's humanity is put on display—worked me into an encompassing melancholy as we explored this important corner of United States history.

It's interesting to think back on the visit. It all felt terribly relevant to today, partly due to the invective and rhetoric on display in our politics of recent time, and partly due to the unnerving sense that we may be moving fast toward a war much more significant than the seven shadow wars we have been fighting in recent (and not-so-recent) years, but also due to the fact that with each passing month, it feels more and more as though this country is sliding down a precipice toward some very harsh and dire times. Throughout my relatively young life, the closest this country has ever felt to an existential crisis was the terrorist attacks of 9/11. While they obviously set us on a new path of destruction that continues today—and perhaps one could point to that attack and the 2008 economic crisis as the two key events that have accelerated and driven, hard, our imperial decline—it feels to me as though we are fast moving toward something larger and more disruptive, toward a break the consequences of which will put both those past events to shame. I've read that prior to World War I, there was a sense across much of the world that something had to break, that the center couldn't hold, and that the beginning of the Great War brought a surprising relief for many people: an understanding, finally, that this was the challenge to be dealt with.

I wonder sometimes if we now are waiting for such a moment of our own. It feels today as though chaos reigns, as though the comfortable certainties of the near past have been pitched into the compost bin and that a great disruption that will remake the shape of our world looms ahead of us. To be honest, I suspect there's truth to that, as foreboding (though also in ways tempting) an idea that is. And yet, while my own intense dissatisfaction with our status quo leaves me yearning for significant disruption and while I feel as though this country remains firmly on an utterly (in so many ways) unsustainable course, I fear what such a disruption might bring. I believe in the good of humanity, but I have no delusions that it doesn't also come with an inexhaustible store of cruelty. Great disruption creates the opportunity for both, and as frustrating and unsustainable as the current status quo may be, there is far from any guarantee that a remaking of our world would be for the better.

As I examined the photos in the Manzanar museum, listened to the oral histories of the camp's internees, walked through replicas of the barracks and latrines, and read alternating tales of human kindness and cruelty, I couldn't help but imagine what a future of truly hard choices brought to us here in America may bring. We already act like a terribly fractured country; do I trust us to come together in times of tribulation, or would I expect us to splinter farther apart and to give in to savage impulses? I don't know that I'm optimistic at this point. We all seem so angry and frightened. So many people have already been pushed up against the wall. Layering additional stress and fear atop all that may take too many of us past the breaking point.

Therein lies so much of my concern for the future. While at the face to face level, I believe humans are more good than bad in times of stress and uncertainty, there is no question that terrible behavior can arise. More importantly, at the collective level it seems as though we all are far too susceptible to manipulation, mob behavior, and a pooled cruelty toward others—particularly toward "the other," which can be defined in an impressively myriad number of ways by those seeking power. Stripped of our comfort and affluence, or of the solidity of the world around us, collective outrages such as the internment of Japanese Americans and Japanese immigrants or the horrific war crimes perpetrated in Hiroshima and Nagasaki become all too plausible.

At such times, there's little question that the decency and generosity of humans comes to the fore, as well. Perhaps it does so even more than the cruelty, though I don't know that I am certain of that. Yet the stories of Manzanar highlight some of that decency, from the internees who volunteered to go the camps early to build their neighbors' eventual home to the non-Japanese American citizens who understood the immorality of the internment camps and sought to help in some way. They confronted a broken world and worked to improve it, often in small ways, hoping to make their slight difference and craft a somewhat better world for future inhabitants. As we continue to slide down our own arc of decline, such a challenge faces us, as well. For now, for many of us, it is a challenge not nearly so dire as the one that arose seventy-five years ago. But it's early yet, and the years to come may prove as hard and critical as those decades past. My hope is that we will do better than we did then; that our susceptibility to cruelty will prove lesser, or that our luck will prove better. My suspicion, unfortunately, is that neither will be the case. And should that bear itself out, my final hope is that we can find the grace, generosity, and kindness that I saw on display in the histories of Manzanar while shying away from the hatred and cruelties I saw in the same. Our choices will one day be our own legacies, whether memorialized in some future museum or not, and I know the kind of legacy I hope to leave. The question is whether or not we will have the character to leave such a legacy, or if we'll succumb to the fear and weakness that will leave a very different type of memory for future generations.

— Portland, Oregon
May 19, 2017

Into the Ruins is published quarterly by Figuration Press. We publish deindustrial science fiction that explores a future defined by natural limits, energy and resource depletion, industrial decline, climate change, and other consequences stemming from the reckless and shortsighted exploitation of our planet, as well as the ways that humans will adapt, survive, live, die, and thrive within this future.

One year, four issue subscriptions to *Into the Ruins* are $39. You can subscribe by visiting intotheruins.com/subscribe or by mailing a check made out to Figuration Press to:

Figuration Press / 3515 SE Clinton Street / Portland, OR 97202

To submit your work for publication, please visit intotheruins.com/submissions or email submissions@intotheruins.com.

All issues of *Into the Ruins* are printed on paper, first and foremost. Electronic versions will be made available as high quality PDF downloads. Please visit our website for more information. The opinions expressed by the authors do not necessarily reflect the opinions of Figuration Press or *Into the Ruins*. Except those expressed by Joel Caris, since this is a sole proprietorship. That said, all opinions are subject to (and commonly do) change, for despite the Editor's occasional actions suggesting the contrary, it turns out he does not know everything and the world often still surprises him.

EDITOR-IN-CHIEF
JOEL CARIS

ASSOCIATE EDITOR
SHANE WILSON

DESIGNER
JOEL CARIS

WITH THANKS TO
SHANE WILSON
JOHN MICHAEL GREER
OUR SUBSCRIBERS

SPECIAL THANKS TO
KATE O'NEILL

Contributors

Catherine McGuire is a writer and artist with a deep concern for our planet's future. She has three decades of published poetry, four poetry chapbooks, and a full-length poetry book, *Elegy for the 21st Century* (FutureCycle Press). A deindustrial science fiction novel, *Lifeline*, was just released by Founders House Publishing (http://bit.ly/2rkTPti). Find her at cathymcguire.com.

Joel Caris is a gardener and homesteader, occasional farmer, passionate advocate for local and community food systems, sporadic writer, voracious reader, sometimes prone to distraction and too attendant to detail, a little bit crazy, a cynical optimist, and both deeply empathetic toward and frustrated with humanity. He is your friendly local editor and publisher. As a reader of this journal and perhaps other writings of his, he hopes you don't too easily tire of his voice and perspective. He lives in Oregon with an amazing, endlessly patient woman whom he can't wait to marry.

G.Kay Bishop is the type of writer who invents words when those in current usage do not suit a concept or have drifted too far from their etymological roots. Bishop also claims to have been issued with the famous Poetic License No. 00013: the License to Spell. Shakespearean scholars have cast doubt on this bold assertion, but what can you expect from people who obsess over a guy who died 401 years ago and stole his plots from Italians? Jane Austen (d. 1817) was also a creative speller who cribbed lots of her ideas from Charlotte Turner Smith. So there!

Dylan Siebert studies history in Kitchener, Ontario. He is a gardener and a cyclist, and looks forward to doing more of both in the future. He enjoys riding buses when the occasion permits. More of Dylan's work can be found online at awizardofearth.blogspot.ca.

Born in the gritty Navy town of Bremerton, Washington and raised in the south Seattle suburbs, JOHN MICHAEL GREER started writing about as soon as he could hold a pencil. He is the author of more than forty nonfiction books and six novels, including the deindustrial novels *Star's Reach* and *Retrotopia*, and has edited four volumes of the *After Oil* series of deindustrial science fiction anthologies. He also wrote the weekly blog "The Archdruid Report" for eleven years. These days he lives in Cumberland, Maryland, an old red brick mill town in the north central Appalachians, with his wife Sara.

W. JACK SAVAGE is a retired broadcaster and educator. He is the author of seven books, including *Imagination: The Art of W. Jack Savage* (wjacksavage.com). To date, more than fifty of Jack's short stories and over seven hundred of his paintings and drawings have been published worldwide. Jack and his wife Kathy live in Monrovia, California. Jack is, as usual, responsible for this issue's cover art.

JUSTIN PATRICK MOORE, KE8COY, is a writer, radio hobbyist and student of the Mysteries. His work has been published in *AntenneX*, *Flurb* and *Abraxas: International Journal of Esoteric Studies*. The various flavors of his writings can be sampled at sothismedias.com. He was on the airwaves for over ten years at community station WAIF 88.3 FM on the shows *Art Damage* and *On the Way to the Peak of Normal*. After being off the air he found he still had the radio bug and acquired a ham license that is providing a new realm of growth and exploration. Justin and his wife Audrey make their home in Cincinnati, the Queen of the West.

MATTHEW PANGBORN is an associate professor of English and writing at Briar Cliff University in Sioux City, Iowa. He co-edits fiction for *The Briar Cliff Review*.

WYLIE HARRIS has been writing practically since he could hold a pencil, but has found that editing comes closer to paying the bills. He lives in Texas.

LETTERS TO THE EDITOR

Editor's Note: In late April, I asked a simple question of Into the Ruins *readers: Given our state of decline and the hard realities of climate change, economic and political dysfunction, war, poverty, environmental destruction, and all the other troubles facing us, what do you hope for? I asked not for fantasies of simple solutions involving abundant new energy sources, miraculous technologies of ecological remediation, vast shifts in human consciousness, or any of the other blind hopes peddled by those unwilling to face the consequences of our collective actions, but instead honest hopes for the future rooted in hard work, realistic evaluations of the world as it is, and unflinching acceptance of our unyielding reality coupled with a determination to make that reality better than it might otherwise be—even if not what we might wish it would be. The following are a few of the responses I received.*

Dear Editor,

As you put it, all of humanity and many, many other species face a very harsh future. The earth is, after all, entering the era of rapid climate change (for the worse, unless you're a cockroach or a jellyfish) and the Sixth Extinction, where twenty-five to seventy-five percent or more of all species are predicted to go extinct. So what can a rational person, a compassionate person, hope for?

This is a very difficult question because humans in the modern era are accustomed to hoping for better times, better outcomes, or that "good times" remain as long as possible. In the United States, it's simply impossible to win any elected office if the candidate does not embrace a mandatory optimism about the future. Who, after all, will vote for someone who says that we face a choice between a very difficult, challenging future and a truly catastrophic one, or even an apocalyptic one that leads to human extinction or a fall back to neolithic levels? How many people even want to have that discussion? Much better to stick with "positive" narratives like "A New Morning in America," or "Make America Great Again." Even "liberal" entities in the U.S. like the Green Party and "centrist" ones like the Democratic Party have their own forms of politically acceptable delusion, all necessary to project an optimistic future where climate change can be moderated, even reversed, and middle class, high energy consumption lifestyles can be maintained. Just sprinkle in electric cars, solar PV panels and windmills, organic agriculture, some fairy dust, and *voila*: Ernie Callenbach's *Ecotopia*.

What can a rational person hope for? Let's define a rational person as someone who's read and takes seriously at least some of the works of John Michael Greer, Richard Heinberg, William Catton, Chris Martenson, Marty Zehner, Bill McKibben, Thom Hartmann, Andrew Bacevich, Jeff Rubin, Michael Klare, Mark Hertsgaard, etc. In other words, someone who accepts in their bones that the human future is going to be far more difficult than almost anyone alive today has ever experienced. Someone who understands that the twenty-first century is going to be "The Century of Malthus" —a century filled with famines, droughts, floods, pandemics, civil chaos, wars.

Such a rational person would recognize that all the options are bad, and some options (like doing nothing at all, letting neoliberal economic values continue to control modern societies) are far worse. In those circumstances, a rational person would have to a) support efforts to insure that the least bad outcomes were the more likely, b) preserve what they consider worth saving and what could survive in a far less complex society, and c) hope that the suffering that will affect billions of people (not to mention entire species that will go extinct) can be minimized.

The next question then becomes: How should a rational person live? This is surely a question readers of *Into the Ruins* wrestle with, the current writer included. In my humble opinion, the guiding principle should be: do no harm, or do as little harm as you possibly can. Most of us cannot live lives like Helen and Scott Nearing (authors of *Five Acres and Independence*). In practice this means: live lightly, consume what you need to live a modest life. Use sustainable energy whenever possible. Eat organic foods when available. Radically reduce meat consumption. Only fly when absolutely mandatory (e.g., funerals). Prefer walking, biking and public transit over single vehicle driving.

Have I personally been a model of living as lightly as possible? Not often enough. But in the words of John Lennon, "We're all doing what we can." What I am most focused on is learning as much as I can about what's going on with the climate, with energy, with human societies and human conflicts, and what can be done politically to push for a "least bad" future.

Ric Steinberger
Incline Village, Nevada

Dear Editor,

A preliminary: I hope that the destructive/extractive industries collapse before our breathable atmosphere does.

I hope to help build a world that cultivates, nurtures, and rewards the dignity of community self-reliance (not to be confused with lone-wolf self-sufficiency). I assume that a world adapted to an unstable climate will necessarily be largely decentralized, mobile, resourceful, and "scrappy." Those communities that learn to work together, keep their eyes open, work hard, be clever, and expect little help from the world at large will tend to survive and thrive. I hope for flourishing and diverse traditions and practices related to successfully navigating an uncertain world.

I hope for a world where culture, art, intellectual pursuit, religion/worldview, story, and craft diverges again into a rich ecosystem. I hope that the rot of certain high technologies re-engages minds with the durable reality of the world.

I hope that the decentralization of power and authority leads to myriad experiments in social/political organization all over the world, and that out of this socio-evolutionary process, systems are found that are not kleptocratic, authoritarian, or dictatorial, but are able to survive and thrive against such.

I hope for the return of vernacular, creative, beautiful architecture that the world has never seen before.

Tyler Disney
Santa Fe, New Mexico

Dear Editor,

I hope to make a difference, that the world will be a slightly better place because of my passage through it. While I understand, in the context of deindustrialization and the long decline, that "the system cannot be saved"—and I will admit this acceptance has been a difficult, emotional, but vitally necessary inner journey for me—I do believe that I can act locally to mitigate the impact upon my community of this storm that is coming, and to aid, if only in some small way, the birth of a renaissance, centuries hence, that I will not live to see.

David England
Two Rivers, Wisconsin

Dear Editor,

In some ways, the future has already arrived here. In September 2015, the massive Butte Fire destroyed 550 homes and burned through more than seventy thousand acres of oak and pine woodlands, mostly in Calaveras County, where I live. The flames were visible on a ridge over my town, San Andreas, for three nights. The fire spread so quickly and our local emergency services are so understaffed that it was initially impossible for sheriff deputies to warn everyone in the fire's path. Some residents found themselves running from the advancing flames with only the clothes they were wearing. It is a miracle that only two men perished because they failed to evacuate.

As bad it is to suffer the terror of near death or the grief of a destroyed home, there are worse things. Those worse things sometimes come in the aftermath of disasters as communities, families and individuals shatter. And those worse things were already happening here even before the fire.

Terror will pass. And, where human connection and resources allow, homes can be rebuilt. But neither the most luxurious house nor the immediate absence of disaster is enough to foster human happiness.

My hopes for the future are informed, in part, by things I witnessed during more than thirty years as a newspaper reporter and editor, the last twelve of which I spent covering Calaveras County. Journalists poke around in government documents. I was well aware that even before the fire Calaveras County consistently had one of the highest (sometimes the highest) suicide rates in California. When I called mental health experts to ask why the suicide rate would be higher here than in nearby cities, they usually identified isolation as a key factor. In other words, the same solitude and open spaces that many newcomers cite as their reasons for moving here can also limit human connection and deepen despair. Those who have decided to leave often said, in part, that their friends were already gone, or that their community had changed. About the same time, changing state and local regulation of marijuana cultivation triggered a land rush. In many cases, people who lost homes in the Butte Fire or who decided to move away for other reasons sold their properties to marijuana growers. This triggered additional cultural shock as working age adults moved to the area. (Retirees make up a large proportion of the population here.) Some longtime residents feel they are being displaced by the newcomers. In the twenty months since the fire, the fire victims who seem to have regained their desire to live are, in general, those who have maintained the strongest sense of connection to other humans, whether through community ties, a church, meaningful work or extended family.

Yet many intact families are also miserable. Some families are plagued by addiction, some by anxiety and depression and some by more severe mental illnesses. Some families are dominated by abusers. But perhaps the most striking characteristic of families in our time is how small they are. Many households have only one or two high-functioning adults, if that. In fact, the two-adult family is promoted as a norm both in popular culture and by the way governments approach property and marriage. Powerful economic forces put enormous pressure on the few high-functioning adults in each family. That, in turn, shortens their lifespans and triggers additional crises when their health fails.

So my primary hope for the future is that a time comes when the default family is something that is much more like a tribe: many high-functioning adults united to support each other in raising children, feeding the tribe and providing a healthy home. My other hopes are related in that they are, I believe, necessary to restore a more vibrant and resilient family life.

The change in family/tribal structure will also change housing. Instead of isolating people with one or two or a handful in each widely-scattered small house, we will need to provide fewer, larger living places. Whether these will be palaces or villages, I don't know. For a long time, we will be making use of what we inherit. But the age of isolating people in tiny apartments and trailers will end.

My second hope for the future is an end to scarcity. Some scholars believe that scarcity is and has been a fundamental condition distorting our species' family structure since the advent of agriculture eight thousand or ten thousand years ago. (Christopher Ryan and Cacilda Jetha make the case for this in their book, *Sex at Dawn*.)

I am not hoping for scarcity to end thanks to the discovery of some implausible endless energy source that would make it possible to farm corn on floating space stations. Instead, my hope is that our species finds some way to regulate itself so that every baby is born wealthy. We also will define wealth quite differently in my hoped for future. It seems obvious that with a small enough world population, there would be enough resources for every child to be assured a lifetime of clean air, open space to run and high-quality food. I don't know what that number is, or how we will get there. The total number of people the planet could support in a truly high-quality life might only be one or two million. Obviously population descent poses incredible challenges. Miserable conditions do not stop people from reproducing or

wanting to reproduce. But the population correction will happen to some extent whether or not our species cooperates. And voluntary, mindful population reduction could immediately improve the ratio of high-functioning adults to children. If there were four or five or eight adults available for every child, everyone would benefit. The children get more attention. The other adults get more companionship. The additional adults act as buffers when someone dies prematurely or has a crisis of some sort.

A deliberate end to scarcity will require us to know our planet and its capacities much more intimately than we now do. It will require us to know the forests and fields and to accurately calculate what we can take without damaging the systems. Tribes managing the local terrain will need to be able to trust and cooperate with other tribes to keep the human impact in balance. Otherwise, the whole vicious cycle of human expansion, empire and conquest will resume.

My third hope is to that we remake our institutions to a more human scale. Again, this will happen whether or not we seek to make it so. The end to cheap and abundant energy will make long supply chains less viable. The revitalization of extended family/tribal life goes hand-in-hand with a post-industrial way of life. Our society is now fractured into specialties. This specialization leads to conflict and exploitation. Our healers are also seeking to make profits by selling us dangerous drugs. Our police don't identify with many of the communities they serve and so behave as an occupying army at times rather than as family peacekeepers. Taking these functions to a tribal level would have benefits. Healers would have their patients' interests at heart rather than corporate profits. Police would treat offenders as family members rather than enemies. One looming question is the extent to which we can preserve records of the vast information available in the present age. We will want to have access to histories of the various branches of human knowledge in the coming age, even when we no longer have electrically powered computers. Can we save a few libraries? Can there still be a few medical schools where tribes can send their candidate healers for training? It seems that we need a population descent plan.

So those are my hopes: tribal families, an end to scarcity, and human-scale institutions. Instead of living in a world crowded with billions of strangers where we hide in our homes, we will live in a world of vast spaces where we have the companionship of a few dozen or a few hundred trusted tribe members. With plenty to eat and leisure time, there will be no reason to neglect our children or our spirits. We will spend a whole lot more time playing, walking, singing, meditating and sleeping. We won't be driving cars.

I've written the first few chapters of a science fiction novel exploring how a future society might emerge that realizes my hopes. It isn't a paradise. And it does assume that humans will make use of bioengineering to address some of their environmental crises. And there is still war. But it consoles me to think that there could be happy people living here in my part of California a century or two from now.

Thanks for asking!

Dana M. Nichols
San Andreas, California

Into the Ruins welcomes letters to the editor from our readers. We encourage thoughtful commentary on the contents of this issue, the themes of the magazine, and humanity's collective future. Readers may email their letters to editor@intotheruins.com or mail to:

Figuration Press
3515 SE Clinton Street
Portland, OR 97202

Please include your full name, city and state, and an email or phone number. Only your name and location will be printed with any accepted letter.

STORIES

THE WORLD GIVEN AND THE WORLD TAKEN AWAY

BY MATTHEW PANGBORN

THE VISITOR FROM THE CAPITAL was youngish and handsome, well-groomed and well fed. He stepped off the cargo plane on its weekly run to the 185th Air Refueling Wing with a smile only slightly tempered by the cold. He was plainly bemused by the rural winter landscape and its eye-watering stench of ammonia. But though his smile was satirical, his fingers' fumbling at his travel pass betrayed his anxiety. The truth was that he had always dreamed himself a person of importance, ever since childhood, and the fact that this errand into flyover country probably represented his last chance at promotion struck him with a humbling irony. And so if he could still gaze on the air base's makeshift office trailer as if from the fragile height of that childhood dream, it was with the expectation of watching that young, self-important boy disappearing, leaving a stranger as old and gray as the senior members of his department, whose talk was only of the interminable hours they put into their work, and the utter lack of pleasure they took from it.

An older man wearing a shabby overcoat met the man and gestured toward an official-looking sedan, shouting something lost in the wash of the jet aircraft just beyond the chain-link fence. The young man nodded politely to his host, hoping he had not missed anything important, and walked alongside his rolling suitcase, wonderingly.

"We'll be meeting with the interviewees in their own homes," the older man said to the visitor, as he swung the groaning car onto the single lane of the pot-holed interstate. "So myself and the Office of Homeland Security would appreciate it if you didn't smile so smugly at them as you did at me just now. We have enough trouble, as a federal entity out here."

The younger man was confused at first, but then felt himself smiling again. "Mr. Pettigrew, I understand people in the heartland may have different ideas than us in the capital, but the only reason I've come out here is to listen to that perspective—"

"Then I'd advise you to start by listening to *me* and dropping the 'heartland' crap. It's bad enough, your wearing such an obviously new suit. You're not going to win your promotion from any of us, you know. Times have been tough, and these people still have a lot of pride."

The younger man searched his memory for reasons he had given his host to be angry with him. It was almost as if the banjo-playing, cousin-marrying jokes he'd traded at the bar with his colleagues the night before had left some kind of evidence. "Everyone has been hit hard," he finally ventured. "Yet your data suggests regional compliance with the FPA is nearly one hundred percent."

"I wouldn't expect that would be cause for sending out Office of Emergency Preparedness staff, frankly," the driver said, with a snort. "Imagine if there were actually an emergency."

The younger man shivered at the gas stations and other small buildings appearing as they approached the small city, all of them shuttered and abandoned, their windows shattered, their walls torn open by repeated searches for wiring, insulation, pipe. "Yes, I expect that is exactly what someone's been doing," he said, and he wrapped his new overcoat more tightly around his chest.

The driver took the next exit off the interstate, and downtown rose before them, no more than a dozen hollowed-out buildings climbing no higher than ten stories, mottled here and there with rust from exposed rebar, the shorter brick buildings patched with cement. As they wound their way through streets cluttered with abandoned cars and random objects—a mattress, a flat-screen television set, an oversized teddy bear—the visitor's eyes widened at the number of storefronts boarded over with graffitied plywood. *Who could live in such a place*, he wondered, *with none of the restaurants and bars of the capital city?* No art, no culture, no money, no beauty. No hope. When the car passed a group of people shouting at one another outside a liquor store, the faces were loud, angry smears, and he was only too grateful to see the car was headed back out of downtown. Soon, they were driving past a city limits sign. Then, the driver abruptly pulled the sedan onto a dirt road, and they swayed to a stop in front of a low, ranch-style house, hemmed in on every side by a corduroy of snow-covered stubble.

"I thought we'd go ahead and get started with the interviews," Mr. Pettigrew said, when the younger man cast him a surprised look. "The Swensons. Ronald, fifty-eight. Barbara, fifty-six. Farmers."

The visitor looked out at the cold. "I thought it was all corporate fields out here, now."

"There're still plenty of folks trying to eke out a living on the edges, even with the rationing of fuel and the other shortages. This land is all they've got, as exhausted as it might be."

When the young man glanced up again, a white-haired couple was standing at the front of the house, squinting suspiciously out at the low gray clouds. They were thin and gaunt, and their grim faces evoked a painting he thought he had seen reproductions of, somewhere. Once inside the house, he found the couple to be polite, if not exactly warm, and as they talked at a small kitchen table next to a wood-burning stove the young man was offered coffee, coffee cake, cookies, more coffee, and homemade candy. They watched closely all that he took from the plate, the older woman wincing slightly, once or twice, when he stretched out his hand.

He enjoyed being offered things, especially things to eat, so he did not mind the attention, or the odd flavors of the treats all prepared in the same Second-Depression way: butter replaced by vegetable oil, cane sugar by a homebrewed corn syrup that tasted residually of baking soda. The "coffee," predictably, was roasted chicory root. He sat upright in his chair, trying to keep the sleeves of his new suit away from the grimy surfaces. He counted at least six mounted heads of bucks on the wood-paneled walls of the nearby den.

"So, you're *against* the FPA now?" he found himself reading aloud from his notes, anxious to be sure. "But you and your neighbors originally supported the measure."

"Why, of course we did," Mrs. Swenson said, with a manner that suggested she found the question's lack of common sense disorienting. She even put a hand up to her hair, as if to make sure of her location. "Everywhere you looked, there were more of *them*, chattering away in whatever language they had brought here. Like the radio was always saying, they could have taken over the country without firing a shot. You tell him, dear."

"Yeah . . . we . . . supported it," Mr. Swenson said.

"And no one had any trouble with limiting a family to two children?"

"Well, no, it's what people had been doing for years," said Mrs. Swenson.

"So, why then do you say you're *opposed* to the law, now?"

Mr. Swenson finally shot forward, with an oddly personal sort of vehemence that startled the visitor. "Well, it's because this is America, young man, and we don't plan to forget it!"

The mounted heads met the visitor's surprise with a glassy indifference. As he walked back out to the car with his host in a north wind so sharp and sere it made his cheeks burn, he puzzled over the couple's answers. At least the old man's outburst was something he could laugh about with coworkers back home—with those who had not been jealous of his finally being awarded a mission, that is. But he wasn't home, yet.

"Isn't there someone who actually knows what's going on?" he asked, once they had settled back into the relative warmth of the car.

It was Mr. Pettigrew's turn to cast a questioning look. "What makes you think they don't know what's going on? They're one of the oldest families here."

The young man did not know how to react to this news. He expected it was obvious the couple were at the very least confused about how to participate in the democratic process. He let his gaze linger on the surroundings, everything the color of cardboard. Although the barren landscape stretched to the horizon, what crept over him was the sense of being boxed in.

Mr. Pettigrew toured the young man around to the other nearby family farms, all of them in varying states of disrepair. He was introduced as "an official sent from the capital to get our opinion," which prompted muttering. But nothing else. The second and third couples' answers were the same as the first's, which panicked the young man. He saw looming in front of him a nebulous shape: a Mystery, or, God help him, a Problem, something he was not used to handling without detailed instructions. But then he reflected he had already arrived at the answer to the most important, if implicit, question he had been sent to fetch. These people were no threat at all to public security, no matter what law was passed. They would only mutter. He stretched out his legs, unworried by whatever greasy surface with which his pants might come into contact, and rewarded himself with another cookie.

But the smile was brief. His eyes alighted on a handprint turkey made out of brown construction paper, affixed to the refrigerator and signed "Tasha."

He interrupted the woman opposite him, "You have a child, Mrs . . ."

"Well . . . we have . . . two, of course," the woman said, after she had followed the young man's gaze. She began to redden slightly around her neck. "As the law allows."

"And where is Tasha right now?"

The color spread up her neck to flush the whole of the woman's face. "At school," she decided, darting a sharp look at her husband.

"But it's almost dark."

"They're . . . they're working on the school play."

The handsome young man from the capital, startled by the obviousness of the lie, and baffled by the pettiness of it, glanced at the plate of treats on the table and realized he was in way over his head. All of the interview subjects had offered him sweets from what he suddenly saw was a common source, someone who had not been able to prevent the first interviewees from taking every available dessert and stupidly offering some of each, so he might recognize them at the other houses, too. That common source, as far as the young man could figure, could only be Mr. Pettigrew.

The young man shivered—he was not experienced in guile. Unlike many of his friends, he did not even play poker. Competition made him nervous. It was too much like work. As they drove to their next appointment, he gazed quietly on the unchanging, worn-out landscape of furrowed fields, hoping that a solution might be handed to him, like another cookie.

At the next intersection of country roads, the car nosed up against a large orange detour sign, and Mr. Pettigrew cursed under his breath. "Maybe we should—" he started.

"Should what?"

"Never mind." He put the car back into gear and continued on.

But the young visitor was fully alert now. Following the signs, they passed more snow-patched hills lined with last year's cut cornstalks, more bare trees, more birds scattering here and there like scraps of trash on the wind. And then the young man found his attention caught by an odd, roughed-up section of field, crossing the road and climbing the neighboring hill. He turned his head to keep it in view: about thirty feet wide, it incorporated into its path broken trees and collapsed fences, even what looked to be a house caved in upon itself.

"Did you see that?" he asked the driver. In a broad swath, as if a giant hand had come down.

But the other man only stared straight ahead. "The county never has any money to finish these damn repairs."

They drove for many minutes without seeing another such feature, so that the young man thought maybe he had imagined it. And then, suddenly, another appeared. The path of torn-up earth cut across their route and ran alongside their road until Mr. Pettigrew, with an audible sigh, took the last detour sign to bump back onto the state highway.

The visitor craned his neck to keep the strange sight in view. What could they be, these paths torn into the land? He did not know, but it was obvious enough Mr. Pettigrew would be no help. At the next house, the young man refused the cookies the woman offered to him, and his mind did not wander. He sorted through his memory for other details he might have missed. Only then did he notice among his dim recollections a photograph that must have escaped Mrs. Swenson's hurried sweep. He could picture it on the countertop, peeking out from a crowd of Precious Moments figurines: a rather pretty blond girl, maybe a senior in high school, with strangely sunken eyes.

When they finished the last interview, it was pitch dark, and Mr. Pettigrew drove them to his house on the edge of town. In the warm bubble of the automobile's interior, the young man turned the mystery about in his mind. The people had all watched him so narrowly, and they had spoken so slowly—one might even say mournfully. As if carefully piecing the world back together after having watched it all fall apart. What had happened, he had no idea. One thing was clear to him, however, and that was the pride his host had asserted was so strong in these people must have been a thing of the distant past.

When they arrived at Mr. Pettigrew's house, they entered through the kitchen door, bumping into Mrs. Pettigrew preparing dinner, and Mr. Pettigrew introduced them. His wife was a very beautiful woman, beautiful enough to make the young man forget his trouble, if only for a moment. Delicately featured and lightly freckled across the bridge of her nose, with soft eyelashes and pale blue eyes, she moved with an introspective grace. She and her husband were of that age at which it was just possible they might be grandparents—which in this region, he expected, meant they probably *were* grandparents, even given the times—but there were no children around their house, either.

At dinner, Mrs. Pettigrew smiled a very fine, if slightly unbalanced, smile, holding her wine glass beside the point of her chin and gazing into the candlelight. "And so why did you enter this line of work—Office of Emergency Preparedness—anyway?"

The young man remarked, with some embarrassment, that he had not been interested in any job after college, but that he had expected he might come to enjoy a position so many other people had wanted, if only because of the puzzles it involved. He had always enjoyed games. He felt himself blushing as he told the woman this, something he had not thought of before.

"And what 'puzzle' brings you out here?"

"Well, it has to do with the Family Protection Act," the younger man said, noticing the way Mr. Pettigrew kept a close eye on his wife. "Everybody here says they have a problem with it, but no one seems to have a problem with it, if you know what I mean. Nothing like in the cities on the coasts, where there's still a protest every week—"

"So, your superiors were wondering why, in agricultural areas, where people actually have a use for large families, there's been no resistance to a law limiting their size?"

"Something like that," admitted the young man, chagrined to find his mission explained more clearly than he himself had understood it. He felt as he always did in such circumstances: resentful that things had to be so complicated, when it must have been plain to all he was trying.

"And did you see any migrating birds, while you were out today?" the woman asked, leaning in, and smiling, as if to distract him from the mood she had read only too clearly. "Ducks? Geese? You can often see great flights of them, this time of year."

The young man blinked. "No, I had not thought of birds—"

"They're beautiful," the woman said, "or, at least, I think so, even though, as you know, they're engaged essentially in a race against starvation. At a distance, they look beautiful. One doesn't have to feel their panicked heartbeat, their straining muscles. Their hunger. They're way up in the sky."

"Please excuse my wife's flair for the dramatic," Mr. Pettigrew said. "She's a bird lover, you know. We don't get a lot of visitors."

The young man stared. "Yes, they told me there were no hotels—"

"Oh, don't worry—we receive a stipend from Adam's office for visitors," Mrs. Pettigrew said, stretching out a thin hand to touch the young man lightly on the arm. "It's not every night we have beef stew. I know it can't be up to city standards, but it's a real treat for us. And I don't know when the last time was we had wine."

Mr. Pettigrew darted a look at his wife.

The young man felt as if he was being made fun of, somehow. He liked the status of his job but not the effort of thought it sometimes required. He didn't know why he'd said he liked puzzles. Puzzles always made him feel stupid. As well, the thin, graceful woman asked him so many questions that he felt as if he were the interviewee.

"So, have people in the capital been affected at all by the hard times?"

"Of course. People have had to conserve what they have, you know, be careful." He was conscious he could not provide any specific examples, and felt flustered.

"It's just that, whenever we have enough power to watch the occasional transmission, everything seems like it's just going on like before. Have *you* suffered, for example?"

"Honey," the older man said.

But the young man was not averse to exploring his own feelings. As the woman might have already guessed, it was relating to other people's that was the challenge.

"It's . . . very competitive," he said. "If you have a good job, you keep it, even if it feels sometimes, maybe, like you're just part of a big machine that will throw you away as soon as it has used you up. I'm lucky, I guess, because I have friends, but it's nothing like how things were when we were in school. There is so little enjoyment in life, nowadays. Don't you think?"

He must have felt he was articulating something wise, because he plainly did not understand his hosts' silence.

"I think we better call it a night," Mr. Pettigrew said, when he saw his wife opening her mouth again.

The woman pressed her lips together. "Let me show you to your room," she said, and the visitor dutifully followed the woman as she slowly, deliberately wove her way up the stairs.

‡‡

But he could not fall asleep.

The Pettigrews had put him in an upstairs bedroom, away from the master on the main floor. In an earlier era, this second story would have been the domain of children, a noisy test-chamber of joyful energy, and the young man was surprised to feel so palpably that energy's absence. He had always felt his own childhood was like a bright dream, one from which he had regretted having to awaken. And he felt, in the abandoned room, a sudden, desperate pull to return.

He looked around himself. Every surface was cluttered in what seemed after that long day a typical Midwestern manner of daring nothing while saying too much. On the wall opposite hung an amateurish painting of a cornfield, with a ragged *V* of beating wings stretched across a purpling sky. There were vases and figurines, framed words of wisdom, antique household items of unrecognizable function, old gimme caps, farm-equipment calendars. But nothing, he came to realize, nothing having to do with children.

He thought he understood then why he had been sent there: his superiors must have realized they had also been lied to. But without the satellites, who knew what was really going on? So, after a long spell of trying to fall asleep, he finally decided to get up and look. There were three other bedrooms, containing a few carpentry tools and building materials. And what appeared to be a small closet, locked. He rustled through the jumble in his room, looking for something of use, and stumbled on a hairpin. Picking the closet door's lock with it took only a few seconds. Inside were shelves crammed with ballet tutus, coloring books and make-up kits, the assorted paraphernalia of at least two little girls.

His heart thumped. He did not go back to the bedroom but kept walking, as softly as he was able, to the head of the stairs. He thought he smelled something burning. After a few steps, he could see a light in the kitchen, a candle on one of the countertops. And after a few steps more, he could make out the broad back of Mr. Pettigrew.

"You opened the closet door," the older man said. He sat with his head down, in the near-dark. The young man wondered what else the older man was hiding, but with two more steps he could see all the man had in front of him was a steaming mug. And the black rectangle of a rare unboarded window.

Mr. Pettigrew turned to face him. "My wife put those things in the closet so you would find them. We normally keep that stuff in the basement. I thought about stopping her, but . . . if you were married, you would understand. They're gone."

"Who's gone?"

"Our girls." Mr. Pettigrew glanced down at his hands and then shifted his attention to the window. "They're out there, somewhere." He got up, and it took all the young man's strength to stand there—not to run, not to prepare himself, somehow, for the attack that must come. But the other man only went to the hot plate hooked up to a small propane bottle and poured what was left of the now-cold pot into another cup. He took the cup back to the table and placed it in front of an empty chair. "Sorry, I expected you more than an hour ago."

After a long moment, the young man realized he was as apt to receive an invitation as he was to be hit, so he went to the chair and sat. The tepid liquid was the same chicory he had drunk earlier: boiled to death, overly sweet from corn syrup, with the same lingering tang of baking soda. But certainly it couldn't have been the same batch.

"You're not a parent," the older man said to the visitor, "so you wouldn't know what the experience does to you, what you have to endure. Ear infections that make them scream for hours in the night. Random objects they try to swallow. The hard edges of countertops, coffee tables. Cars. Stairs. Strangers.

"And, at the same time, you can't hide anything from them. They see everything, and they reflect back what you give them—like little mirrors—"

"Did someone take them? Is that what this is?"

The older man lifted his face, and the young man from the capital finally noticed the wrinkles around his eyes, the looseness of the skin under his square jaw. A suppressed mood of deep sadness and desperation. On the countertop nearby sat a mason jar half full of a colorless liquid. Mr. Pettigrew followed the visitor's gaze.

"Moonshine. A guy at the office distills it. Do you want any? No, of course you don't. When it started, you see, it seemed to be something going on in the cities. Things went to hell, and all of a sudden all of the kids seemed to have gone wild, too. People noticed, of course, but they never thought it would touch us, here."

The wind outside rustled a tree up against the window, making the young man jump.

"It's not enough to provide our children with rules, keep them safe," Mr. Pettigrew said. "The world we give to them has to make sense."

The young man stared.

"You don't understand," the older man said. "But what if I showed you?"

"Showed me what?"

Mr. Pettigrew directed his gaze back to the window. "Just . . . just wait here, for a moment. Maybe tonight is the night."

The visitor from the capital sat with his host for a long while, turning over the conversation in his mind and staring at the black rectangle of the window, anxious that at any moment someone would come. Then, he heard a sound he could not place, and he realized the other man was softly snoring. If what the young man was faced with here was a puzzle, he decided, he must have been missing an important piece. He crept back upstairs and under the covers of his child's bed, leaving his host to complete his mysterious vigil all by himself.

‡‡

Only when he decided he would try to leave the next day was he able to relax. To hell with what quitting would do to his vision of promotion—one of his co-workers was welcome to his job, which, frankly, he had to admit he was not very good at. He had only scored well on the tests. He would return, tell them he was finished, and he would be free of the dreary old department, somewhere far away from its complaining and backstabbing. And somewhere far away from this barren, depressing wasteland. Where exactly that would be would take care of itself, he wanted to believe.

And it worked. Finally, he fell asleep. And instantly, the handsome young man from the capital dreamed. He was standing in the middle of one of the county roads he and Mr. Pettigrew had traveled that afternoon, the gravel crunching under his new shoes. A hill to one side of the road tilted up, just like a book, and standing right next to it was Mrs. Pettigrew, perfectly naked, pointing at some marks that had been dug into the soil.

"Are you okay, Mrs. Pettigrew?" he wanted to ask her, but something about her expression stopped him. She was trembling all over, so that even her head was shaking. He resisted the urge to go to her, noticing that her pale beauty was marred here and there by a strange bruising. He felt himself staring and averted his eyes to the ground. The lines dug in it made letters.

"What does it say?" he asked her. She did not answer. "What does it say?" he repeated, and suddenly her trembling face was up next to his own.

A flight of geese soared overhead, in a confused jumble, calling out with a laughter of children.

He woke up then, all alone in the strange, darkened room. A skinny sliver of moon peeked through the curtain. He tried to raise a hand to rub his eyes but found that he had lain on his arm wrong and it would not move.

When the young man awoke again, it was well past noon. He was not conscious of having been so tired, and he gazed with skepticism at his antique watch, a graduation present from almost a decade ago, now. He twisted the winding knob and brought the little machine to his ear: shh shh, shh shh. The sunlight streaming in through the curtains made a warm patch on top of the comforter. He rested his hands in it for a while. Then he dressed and went downstairs.

Someone had left a carafe of what they called coffee, and a cinnamon roll. It was smaller than he would have wished, but it looked like it would have to do, because there was nothing else. Next to the pastry was a note that read, *Back in a little while.*

He ate breakfast while trying to get reception on his phone. But he had no luck getting the phone to work, so he turned it off again, having no place to recharge it. Then, he found himself staring at the open front door of the two-story house across the street. It looked like a mouth, ready to say something. The young man watched the open door for a long time. But nothing came out.

He heard a door slam and footfalls make their way to the stairs.

From the top, he could see Mr. Pettigrew looking up at him. "I said some things last night," he started. He held up a hand to keep the younger man from interrupting. "I intend to keep the promise I made to you, of showing you what is going on."

"How?" The visitor did not feel ambitious anymore. Or even curious. He was only conscious he was not in control of what would happen next.

The older man watched his expressions. "I want you to come for a ride with me."

"When?" the young man asked.

The older man smiled. "Right now."

They drove north out of the city this time, instead of east, staying along a backbone of hills close to the river rather than heading out into the more gently rolling countryside where the great corporate farms were. The young man kept in sight the hands of the man driving. It was clear there was something wrong with the people here. And he could not help but wonder if his superiors had come to the same conclusion. Had he been picked for this errand because they thought him expendable? He felt like the worm upon the hook. When the car took a sharp turn, he took special pains to keep Mr. Pettigrew under observation, following his hands across the wheel and then back again.

This continued for some time. Then, they stopped at a farm. Mr. Pettigrew got out but did not invite the young man to get out with him. He spoke to another, older man, his face creased with worry and weather, both talking at the cold, gray horizon. Then Mr. Pettigrew got back into the car, and they drove on to the next place, where the pattern repeated itself. The young man pulled his new woolen overcoat closer around his chest.

Toward dusk, they came to a stop at a farm where the figure that came out to greet them was not of a man but rather a thin, angular woman with long gray hair tucked up under a baseball cap. Mr. Pettigrew went out to talk to her, and this time they did not look at the horizon. They looked at each other. The woman pointed, her breath trailing off in torn clouds. It seemed to the young man that she was pointing at the barbed-wire fence on the other side of the road, but he could not be sure. She could have as easily been gesturing toward the furrowed field, or the leafless trees on the other side, one emptiness or another. Only, one thing he understood, and that was she was pointing out danger.

Mr. Pettigrew came back to the car, opened the door, and leaned in. "Okay. This is it."

The young man didn't ask what "it" was. And Mr. Pettigrew did not offer to explain. He only closed the door and went to join the woman. They began walking to the farmhouse. When they did not glance back at him, the young man had a vision again of the woman's gesture of warning, and he decided he should hurry to catch them up.

They walked in through a side door and into the kitchen, hardly any warmer than outside. They kept on their coats. The woman waved the two men toward a small round table with four plastic chairs, and Mr. Pettigrew and the young man sat down. The woman went around a bank of cabinets hanging over a countertop and came back with three steaming mugs.

"So, you're here to report on what's happening. Is that true?" the woman asked.

Mr. Pettigrew interrupted to introduce them, describing the young man as "from the capital" and the woman, Kate, as "a farmer."

"My husband was the farmer. I'm just carrying on, as best I can." She added, for the young man, "He died, just as all of this mess was beginning. We had four sons—plenty old enough not to need grandfathered in. My sons and I saw what happened to so many of our neighbors' children, and then . . ."

She paused over her mug. The young man did not dare drink anything, himself.

"People here were hit really hard by the Crash. I don't think it's possible for you to imagine. Some said it was like something out of the Bible. Others, like something out of a horror film. The first winter, people weren't prepared. An agricultural area, you might think that . . ." She hesitated. "There were awful stories that went round."

"Unsubstantiated stories," Mr. Pettigrew said, gruffly. "Rumors."

The woman turned to him, with a look of anguish. "You know as well as I do there was truth to enough of them. You had to have seen things, just like I saw things. Just enough—"

"Nothing was ever proven," Mr. Pettigrew reminded her.

The woman smiled sadly. "Because there were no resources left to prove them. What would it have mattered? It was all already done. What remained was dealing with the effects."

Outside, the sun had faded to a dull orange behind a windbreak of green conifers. The young man watched the two of them. He had a feeling of unreality, as if the conversation were in some way staged.

"Afterwards, it seemed a sickness was going through the region," the woman continued. "The time in my memory is dimmed, as if there were no days, only a night, everywhere. That's what it seemed like. No one came out of their houses, except to beg, or to barter—quickly, on the street corners, or on people's porches. But what did they have? What did anyone have? Everything went so quickly. The young went quickly."

She looked away. "And those who had lost them did not mention their names. They only withdrew into themselves."

The young man realized he could no longer see her eyes but was staring into a shadow across from him. "Shouldn't we light some candles?"

"No," the woman said. "Definitely not."

"You still want to do this?" Mr. Pettigrew asked her.

"I want to see them for myself. I want to know, once and for all."

"But the cost?"

"Fuck the cost!" the woman shouted. She whimpered quietly, hit her hand on the table top, and then hugged herself for a long time. "I'm sorry," she said.

And when she seemed calm again, the other man asked, "Was Frank sure about their location?"

She was slow in responding. "As sure as anyone can be about anything, these days. All of the Mercers' place, wiped clean. That's just twelve miles down the road." The woman tilted her head for a second at a distant sound. "Just a minute. I think I hear one of my girls."

"Cows—in the barn," Mr. Pettigrew explained, when the woman had gone. "Not many left around here.

"Molly—my wife," the older man continued, "she said I shouldn't take you out in search without explaining. So, here's the only thing I can think to say: whatever you experience here tonight will be real. You understand? You're going to doubt the things you see. But don't make the mistake of thinking that just because you don't believe it, it can't be so."

The young man waited for the older man to tell him what he meant and was so astonished when he just stopped that he found himself perfectly silenced. A dog howled outside, and as soon as its howl had died off, the woman came back, carrying a candle.

"Those cows are all I got left," she said, by way of explanation. "Hell, I think they might be the last ones left in a fifty-mile radius. I hope to God they won't take them. I know what they're up against, but I know what I'm up against, too."

The young man thought he saw the woman look at the other man, but the light from the candle was too faint to be sure. He wondered if her expression were a signal, and he glanced toward the front door. Was there someone out there?

"I think now about how they watched us, even in the most ordinary moments," the woman said to the other man, both of them shadows now in the dark. "We must have appeared to them as monsters, even before it all began. A people of insatiable hunger—"

The dog that had howled earlier let out a wounded yip. The woman lifted up the candle then, and the young man could see her set her head to one side, to listen. Beyond the cry of the dog was another sound, like the scratching of insects.

"Be calm," Mr. Pettigrew said, gently, with a quaver in his voice. He took a revolver from his jacket pocket and laid it on the table. "We'll be fine if we just sit here and don't try to interfere. Just remain still and quiet."

The young man did not know what they were planning, but he would not be caught by surprise. He stood up and backed away from his chair, to keep both of them in view.

The woman hissed. "The worst you can do is get excited. There's too many of them, now. They might—"

"Might what?" said the young man, finally, no longer able to restrain himself. He heard his voice crack. The sound outside was growing in intensity. "I'm expected back home at the end of the week, you know. They will send someone after me if I don't—"

"To who—what are you talking about?" the woman hissed. "Don't you understand what's happening? Don't you understand?"

"You have to stop, be calm," the older man whispered. "*They* are out there!"

The young man backed away from the man with the gun, toward the kitchen door. He turned to go down the steps. They were shaking at the sound that was growing all around, like a thrashing of trees' limbs in the wind. Like the gnashing of teeth.

"Come back, you fool!" the other man called out from inside the house. "What are you doing?"

Outside, the wall next to the young man began to tremble. He felt everything tilt suddenly to one side. In the glow of the candle he had taken from the table swung into view the face of a beautiful, sunken-eyed girl.

He smiled then, the young man from the city. He had never been so scared. "I'm one of you!" he shouted. "I'm on your side!" He had the sense of speaking a piercing truth, finally, of letting out a feeling pent up in him since long before he had arrived. He reached out his hand in the darkness for the girl, for her to take it in her own, but he felt instead his knuckles graze a jagged edge of teeth, and a flat surprise came over his handsome, childish features as he realized even this dream would be taken away from him.

The Wizard of Was

by G. Kay Bishop

SOMETHING WAS DEFINITELY WRONG WITH THE BURNER. Now it flickered too low, giving out intermittent spurts of sickly flame, but if you so much as touched the fuel-feed valve, it would shoot out a great flaming gout, way too high, threatening to set the balloon fabric on fire. He was forced to use a small cast iron skillet to moderate the thing, keeping a constant eye on the nozzle tip and capping it when the flame burst too high while he used the other hand to fiddle with the fuel-feed knob. It was surprisingly tiring to lift the skillet over and over again, to act with a half-second's warning, to get the metal pan into position just so, where it would deflect the flame without either singeing his hand or setting fire to the stays. It was happening so often now that the heat was beginning to come through his improvised hot pad. It was like bailing out a leaky dinghy, except in fire, not water. What would happen when he was too tired? A second too slow, an angle too far off and that's all she wrote. How long could he last? What if he fell asleep at the wheel?

These and many other questions were rendered moot when the fuel assembly simply sputtered and went out. Never to go again. Unpredictable. Inexplicable. He was in the hands of the Gods.

Dispassionately, as becomes a man of science, he considered the ways and means by which he was likely to meet his end. Death was all but certain; what form would it take? He was, at this moment, crossing over a vast desert of a pinkish cast. Had he studied geology instead of anthropology, perhaps he would now know where he was. But the geologist was dead, as were all the others on this expedition. Now he was alone. They had at least died in the company of fellow men, if not fast friends. What was to be his own fate? The lonely death of any explorer whose luck has run out.

Not that he was especially hardy compared to the rest. It was only by luck that he had been back at camp during the savage attack of the Harvester bandits. Had he been in the field, as planned, he would have been left behind. He never knew what the bandits were after, exactly. Slaves? Supplies? The dirigible itself? Although the ambushers killed the captain and the two marines, he and the rest managed to lift off in the balloon just in time.

Seven hops later, he and most of the science team had survived the fevers that took the medics almost to a man. But at that point, the mechanics and drilling crew had panicked and mutinied. Fevers rampant, no medical team, going ever farther from help . . . They coerced the co-pilot at gunpoint to return to Base. If they, the science team had not retained ground-based radio comm, the mutinous crew might have killed all of them instead of abandoning the team in the remote wilds.

As it was, the meckos knew we could alert Base and they would be caught. So they simply jettisoned the cargo, the heavier drills, and the back-up equipment and took the risk of flying the ship as far as the Lakes, using up all the fuel to outrun pursuit. We speculated that they meant to abandon the dirigible and ship out on Lake steamers as undocumented cheap labor. Or scavenge around the slum settlements as able-bodied tramps. Who knows? They might even have succeeded in obtaining a pardon if they returned the airship intact, and the valuable drill team alive.

But we were expendable. They knew no one would come to rescue us. Not economical. Plenty more like us, panting for a chance to go out with a drilling crew. Their defiance of the company rep's authority marooned us with only the balloons and half the supplies. We could either all make our crippled way back, or just . . . go on. We all dared to keep on going. For mixed motives. Duty, the chance of profit, whatever. Some—the best!—for the sake of science and sheer curiosity.

Short hops brought the balloon forward to scout the way. The radioman guided us below. Meanwhile, most of us made our way on foot and by titanium canoe through the watery wilds. It was slow going. It was also replete with mosquitoes, leeches and snakes. Most of which we managed to avoid. But not all.

The meteorologist and the sponsor's rep were both middle-aged (indeed, almost elderly) women of considerable bulk and authority, both with a brusque, military manner. Jack had attributed to each a cold, emotionless sterile character, quite devoid of womanly tenderness until they perished of the raging pneumococcal pleurisy. Only after they had succumbed, within hours of one another, did he re-examine his initial impressions, revise his assessment and conclude that they had been lovers all along.

The navigator, the radioman, the geologist, and he, Jack, had decided to press on. With only the four of them, all could fit into the main balloon and carry the fuel and supplies in the smaller dog boat. The navvy used some of the fuel reserves to inflate the dog boat's bladders and get it fully airborne.

Then they were off! Four young men, in the prime of life, full of vigor and free, all on their own, far from the dull routines of manual labor, using their brains. And with a wide open wilderness before them. The radioman and the navvy were like a couple of kids, giddy at the prospect. Even the staid geologist had a faraway look in his eye.

It wasn't the wealth that would have been theirs if they did find the fabled tar fields or discovered a newly thawed reservoir of sweet crude. It was the excitement of exploration.

Whatever fever got the rep, it was something different that killed the other three. Something poxy. Before the burner started acting up, he had only just jettisoned the last of the corpses, saying a few appropriate words for each dead man before hoisting him perilously over the side to rest in whatever peace his spirit could find. Why had he been spared? Perhaps because he and his parents had been exposed to so many pathogens already that he was now immune?

The mission, such as it was, was now his alone. He felt both stern and solemn, lost and found.

Without the burner, he would lose altitude. What else could he safely jettison? On he sailed, all day, and into the moonlit night. He kept trying for a while, then abandoned himself and his fate to the winds.

Fog . . . turbulence . . . PBL? (planetary boundary layer) . . . losing altitude . . . slow descent . . . tar flats—real! . . . methane clouds . . . backpack, essentials . . . parachuting into a lake by moonlight . . . no, not lake, a mud flat . . . burner spark . . . balloon and dog boat going up in fiery ruin . . . crawling to band of trees . . . know no more—

First he saw a group of adult men, all wearing rounded, half-barrel-like straw baskets held up by flat-woven string suspenders. This peculiar garment swung wide and stiff around their midsections, their skinny legs projecting from the bottom edge like the clapper of a handbell.

Ding, dong, bell, he thought, smiling to himself at the odd substitute for a traditional buckskin loincloth. They did not appear to be hostile; neither spear nor blowpipe nor any other projectile weapon was in their hands. What had any man to fear from men who could not kill a deer? Small and thin, too. Weaklings, he judged them, coolly.

His senses of height, strength, security, and humor helped him to smile outwardly as well, a light, engaging smile, neither too submissive nor too forced a grimace: the smile of one who comes in peace and who is no threat to anyone. He spread his arms wide and showed them his empty, weaponless hands. They stared at him, unspeaking and unblinking. Of all the tribal groups he had studied, this one's initial response to a stranger was unique. He felt a rush of exhilaration. Here, at long last, he was truly facing the Unknown.

The barrier of basket-clad men parted to allow another person to come through. They all cast down their eyes before her. She was a young female.

The lower half of her body was clad in a long, tent-like skirt (a ceremonial garment, perhaps?) made, apparently, of fresh leaves stitched together by their own long stems. It looked stiff, clumsy, awkward, quite as comical as the men. He almost laughed but controlled his initial reaction very well. The upper half of her was clad only in a cloud of living butterflies. Without realizing it, he gasped at the sight. Nothing could have been more beautiful. Not even the evening gown of radiant LED sequins he had once seen on an old vid from before the Indtimes.

She beckoned to him to follow. Warily, he obeyed. He kept a distance of five armlengths between himself and his guide. When she stopped, he stopped. When she plucked a fruit, he plucked a fruit.

But he did not eat. He put the fruit into a cloth bag and carried it with him. His demeanor was calm, modest, eyes downcast, respectful. He wanted his body language to convey that he was entirely trustworthy. He knew—he *felt*—that he was being watched. His guide led him on and on deep into the forest. He knew nothing of the way back but he did not care. Here he had found something much more important than a new source of oil.

The density of vegetation was comparable to the island remnants of the Brazilian rainforest before it had been levelled in an ill-advised attempt to grow genetically modified wheat strains that were supposedly immune to the UG99 blight that starved the bread-eating places of the world. The failure of the wheat crops, followed by waves of similar failures in GM corn, rice and even millet had rendered most of the Amazon basin into a sterile plain of cracked hardpan, now used as a vast parking lot for cattle fed by sugarcane and denatured clover bales delivered via hydrogen-lift airships. He remembered the stark terror of being lost in the jungle. He was but a boy then, with his parents who soon responded to his cries. He was safe, in his mother's arms. It was a good memory.

Now, he was lost again, but he still had that figure of a woman before him, leading him, guiding him to safety. He was a man now. He had no fear.

She topped a slight rise and vanished going down the other side. He followed, still cautious. Being much taller than she was, he was able to see over the lip of the hollow before she crossed it. There was something—a group. No, it was a whole village. Stick and vine structures. Flat tops. Sleeping platforms? Rain shelters? He did not know but he would soon find out.

Gazing back at him were some dozens of people, a whole village of people doing villagey things: giving and receiving massage, eating, cooking, tumbling, playing with string toys, weaving, pounding up mash, all kinds of labor-intensive activities. In every stage of undress. At least eighty percent of them were female. Half of those were pregnant or nursing. He had never seen so much fertility in one place in his whole life.

He had penetrated into a wall-less fortress of femininity. That's how it hit him: he was all the way inside an edible brush forest, a garden of paradise, filled with nubile, naked women. The blood rushed from his head so fast he almost fainted on the spot.

He stumbled but caught himself and stood tall and upright for a moment. Then he walked firmly down the slope to meet a new people.

Everyone fled from him. He stood still at once and remained passive, accepting his isolation. He took the fruit he had gathered from his cloth wallet and placed it on the ground, then backed away to a safe distance. He sat on his haunches as the village elders in Brazil had done. He waited. After a long while, an old, old woman came forward and ate of his fruit offering.

Everyone else kept a long distance from him, except the old woman. Never saying a word, she served him and kept him company. She prepared his food, groomed his head and beard, fetched water, removed snakes from his bedding straw and mended his thatched shelter against rain. She seemed wholly devoted to his service, doing nothing besides keeping her eyes fixed on him all day, every day. Sometimes he woke on a full moonlit night to find her staring at him in his sleep.

She was the only female he was allowed to observe openly. For all others, even girl children, he was expected to lower his eyes and to carefully shade them if a young woman came into view. He obeyed this rule scrupulously. He got to know the looks of the old woman very well indeed. She was hideous, with thin sagging flaps of dried-up breast, wide-splayed hips, thick thighs, and practically no waist. Her buttocks were wrinkled and stringy as the rest of her arms, legs and corrugated belly. He supposed that a serving woman was of lower status and so not entitled to the marks of respect. Once, he had shaded his eyes before her, trying to show respect (for really, he did feel a little ashamed) and she had slapped his hand down, almost angrily. It was the only time she ever corrected him.

For three long months he assumed she was his permanent servant or willing slave until he awoke one day tied down to stakes with cords made of a tough, fibrous vine or braided string of hair. She ignored his distress and set about stimulating his genitals until he ejaculated. She sniffed his ejaculate and even tasted it before she grunted to the watching crowd and shrugged. The men of the tribe then came forward and released him. They still never spoke to him, nor made any attempt to learn his speech, but went about their daily business in silence when he was nigh. Sometimes, from a far distance, he caught sight of them conversing among themselves with many hand gesticulations and eager faces, but never when he was near enough to hear what was being said.

He lived among them peaceably taking notes and singing to himself. If he hoped that they would exchange songs with him, he was disappointed. He was fairly frustrated by their unwillingness to communicate, but he remained patient and even thrilled by his discovery of these primitive people.

Besides, what else had he to do? Without these folk, he would be dead by now. Life for him meant nothing except the opportunity to record all he could of their way of life. Everything about these people fascinated him. Not even when he learned, much later, that the garment of living butterflies was created by smearing the torso with a mixture of urine, elk dung and water to attract the insects did the sight lose its initial grip on his imagination.

He knew these were good people by the way they treated their defectives. Some of the men were not small in body but very much so in mind. These large hulking figures—his own size, more or less—seemed less in height because of their stooped shoulders and shuffling, shambling gait. They were like others he had seen in his travels where a too-limited gene pool had produced simpletons or microcephalic infants had been born in places where dangerous pesticides had permeated the soils.

These fellows were not microcephalic. They drooled a bit, but had the sweetest smiles and gentlest temperaments. Their larger frames and heavier muscles made digging in the fields easier for the others. They were always willing to help and seemed happy as the children, though less able to help themselves. The adults were as kindly towards them as could be, helping to feed them, teaching them string games to the best of their more limited abilities, and grooming their more abundant dry and shaggy hair. They seemed like pet bears, large teddy bears to the children who climbed on them like monkeys, perhaps for the fun of being up high or to collect fruit from higher up on the trees.

They did not speak but uttered grunts and wowing noises like dogs to accompany him when he sang. They seemed unable to learn his songs but clustered near him when he sang. Their inept attempts at making music seemed to pain the women, and the men led them away from him when they made these noises. They also had to be guided by children or adults to the latrine areas, which were changed every four months or so. A very sensible practice, suited for the tropics. Urination-only latrines were close to the camps, for the convenience of the pregnant women, no doubt. Fecal latrines were farther off, out of the range of crawling infants and not likely to be stumbled into by the poor defectives.

Ten months from his arrival, a group of young men gathered around him. It must be time for his initiation into the tribe, he thought. He was more than willing. As a full-fledged man, he must have access to the females, as did other men. They surrounded him and almost hustled him to a wide river where a burnt-boat dugout was waiting with two polemen inside.

As if he were a boy rising into puberty, Jack was bidden, with gestures, to strip himself of all his clothing. He obeyed. Then he was urged, still silently, to get into the boat. He obeyed. To be seated. He did so. He was taken to an island where he met an old man—an old, old, *old* man. He wore a loincloth of woven hair, smooth and oiled. Some precious nut oil. Obviously, he must be a special chieftain.

Immeasurable was Jack's surprise when the old man began to speak to him. In perfectly good Canadian.

"You think, perhaps, that we are primitive savages. But we are not. We are scientists, like you. No, don't speak. You are here to learn. We have very little time for me to convey to you what you must know before I die."

The thousands of questions Jack wanted to ask bubbled up, fizzed, and died on his lips. He listened intently to the Elder. His year-long isolation made him hungry to hear every word.

"You are not the first man to come to Foggy Bottom. Yes, you smile. Believe me, the irony of the name does not escape us. This land, like so much that science has tried and failed to encompass, is a place of wonder and mystery and delight; yet it has been given a comic name and an evil repute. So it was with our initial research projects. Let me repeat: you are not the first man to come into Foggy Bottom. I was.

"Before that, the place was a military research site dedicated to understanding how to dominate and control women without the use of language. The funds came from China, the expertise from German and Swiss expatriates, the subjects, all female infants, chiefly from Africa and the Philippines. Canada supplied the land and received the money and said nothing. Yes, it began as an unlawful and unethical isolation chamber experiment of the worst kind. Do not look so shocked. From such a beginning, see now the end! Listen and learn my son.

"You are too young to remember the way the world was back then. The Chinese had saved themselves from starvation by a one-child policy, but their prejudice against girls meant that millions of girls were aborted or abandoned so that each family could have its one child be a son. Naturally, they ended up with a surplus of young men who could not find a bride of breeding age.

"But China flexed its manly muscles and prepared to engage in world war to achieve the dominance denied to them by the Western world's premature forcing of their markets. Economic rape was now to be met with political rape and conqueror rape in occupied territories. They threw their millions of surplus young men into battle, never doubting that many would die, but confident that the survivors would establish Chinese world dominance for three centuries at least. They reckoned without sufficient consideration of the plagues.

"The Western world, jealous of its failing grip on material prosperity, faced with impotence in its quest to pump yet more oil from dried-up beds of post-Cambrian shale, devoted its last efforts to create genetically modified parasites, transcription-scrambling bacteria and synthetic viruses designed to obliterate people of Asian, Hispanic, and African skin colors. You know the results."

Jack nodded, sadly. It seemed that GMO pathogens were color-blind and indiscriminate. Equal opportunity depopulation. Women died in shocking numbers. Infants, far more.

"We have read the journal you are keeping. We know that your parents were missionaries of a faith that secretly advocated and practiced polygynous marriages. Their scientific credentials were impeccable; their outer appearance conformist with liberal values. But their hidden aim was to colonize the minds of the last remaining reservoirs of plague-resistant humanity with their religion. Did you wish to speak? Remember, we haven't much time."

Jack swallowed his indignation and submitted to the slur. It might have been true. How would he know? His father was dead of the Ballistic Buboes. His mother died in a hormone-supported, synthro-womb surrogate childbirth at age sixty-two.

"I, however, started innocently enough with pure research into the origins and ur-function of the female mammalian orgasm, and went ski-sliding rapidly downhill from there. I too was corrupted by the money. The money was incredible," he said, shaking his head slowly, as he paused to recollect.

A little silence held Jack spellbound. But the old man did not expatiate on how it felt to be rich. He seemed unwilling to go on. Finally, he girded his loins, overcame his reluctance, and told the truth.

"But I never got the cash I was promised. The company profits all went to men higher up or to the military. Instead, I was promised free access to any female I desired. All of them, if I liked. I was young," he said, apologetically, "and simpleminded where politics were concerned.

"Once I had agreed to such an immoral bargain, they had me by the balls. I could neither oppose them nor escape. They could ruin my career or have me killed as a traitor any time they chose. I was their slave. What else could I do? I did my work as best I knew how. Forgive me. I know I could have chosen death over dishonor. But by then, the whole enterprise of science was governed by venal motives. I only did as my peers were doing. I knew no better. I was in love with life. And I loved having sex. A man like me—bony, sickly, mild, timid, inclined to be reverent—had little success in dating women."

Jack secretly rejoiced in his own hardy frame and decidedly handsome features. But he kept his mouth shut about it.

"It had long been known by pre-western cultures that giving a woman pleasure during the act of penile intromission improved the chances of conception, even if they did not know the exact biochemical correlates of the matter. Nor did they know of the existence of the Mater. Ah! Mater materialia, Mater magnifica, Mater munifica! Bless our days and guide our ways through the night with the flight of the dove! Even me, a sinner, She fashioned into the instrument of Her will!

"The infant girls who were the subjects of our studies seemed infinite in supply. Disasters and wars worldwide left plenty of orphaned girls and rape-impregnated women whose children we could steal while telling the mothers their children died post-partum.

"The Chinese had a triple motive in kidnapping girls from Muslim countries where genital cutting was the cultural norm. They felt, if obscurely, their own guilt in the footbinding practices they themselves had encouraged and still do in their darkest hours. Rescuing girls before their pleasure tissues could be cut off—sans anesthesia—gratified their collective psyche. Then they could marry the girls to their war veterans and claim the lands in Africa that plagues had depopulated. So long as the girls were born in Africa, the UN allowed them to exert ancestral rights and indigenous claims to re-occupy the land. So the Chinese gained land and racial expansion at the same time. Feminist groups did the dangerous work of infiltrating the countries and stealing the children. They were, of course, never told that the girls were sold to us.

"I dare not tell you of the brutality experienced by our control subjects. I am too ashamed. It was called the Pimp-n-Chimp Lab. Men laughed about it. Soldiers enjoyed it. Despite a direct order, I refused to participate in the rape trials. I nearly lost my life by that decision. It is the only part of that time of my life that I am proud to remember. The faces of the men who could not force me to become as low as they. How they hated me!

"After that, I was only kept alive for one reason: my frozen sperm was ten times more viable than the fresh sperm of the men who carried out the rapes. No," he said, forestalling Jack's derisive comment, "it is true. During my trial, the data was entered into the records. The Harpie Commandos showed me the actual memos.

"We were obliged to give sperm samples as a condition of our employment; it was supposed to be for security and forensic reasons. In truth, it was a ploy to obtain unlicensed genetic material for secret experiments. It was used without my knowledge or permission. Not only the experimental subjects but also the badly abused women were eight to ten times more likely to conceive from my sperm and to carry to term eggs spliced with selected portions of my genetic material. This is the only reason I am alive today. I am not proud of this fact. It was the Hand of the Mater who preserved me.

"The battered women lost ninety percent of their offspring to plagues. Epigenetics led to the reasons why: chronic disease tendencies were activated by methylation related to the adverse living conditions. But offspring whose mothers were given pleasure thrived. What we discovered, among many other things, was that if a female experienced orgasm during coition, certain cascades of hormonal flow primed the womb for conception. But that was not all, by a long chalk."

A long tale followed in which the old man detailed the extraordinary sequence of cures they discovered by reducing maternal stress, instituting daily massage, providing meals to pregnant women, waiting on them hand and foot, and many other pleasure-based initiatives.

"Under the care of our secret laboratories, our women's resistance to diseases new and old increased by leaps and bounds. Among the causes of constant birth rate attrition among the general population were neo-species of hantavirus; newly crafted germs carried by eider ducks, wild pigs, and foxes; mutant forms of anthrax, anaplasma capra, and cattle abortion; several neo-spirochetes, and sexually transmitted Ebola-related and Zika-mutant pathogens.

"Our isolation had protected us from most strains of germ tissue carrying plasmid-mediated resistance to colistin. But by bad luck for the Masters—that was what they called themselves, do not blame me—horizontal transfer from an Enterobacter cloacae to one of our experimental cultures—a pork eater brought it in—was set loose among our subjects. So many subjects died that we had to step up our involuntary recruitment to replenish the breeding stock. This was a serious mistake.

"The spike in the rate at which girls were disappearing alerted women to the existence of our labs. Word spread. Discovered at long last by certain feminists, our doom was upon us. They infiltrated us as easily as they did the Muslim cultures. Their vengeance was swift and terrible. I helped. In exchange for my life. And to continue my work. My son, the work was all that counted in the end. The work was important, not me. I was but the tool of the Mater.

"The world's population was by then so depleted that even the Harpies of women's avenging armies felt our illicit work must go on. Just as Americans took in Nazi rocket scientists and used them to develop the space program and cow the world with nuclear might, so too did the Canadians hope to use our research to govern the world with a burst of new fertility.

"After the limited nuclear exchanges, women's fertility was more important than ever. All animals were at risk, not just those who weighed twenty-five kilograms or less. Radiation effects yielded monsters everywhere from every species on earth. By now, we were bonded in a sisterhood of hope and our babies were growing up strong and healthy. Mater guided us and held us in the palm of her hand.

"We followed the thin, faintly ridiculous thread of women's orgasms down into hormonal cascades, down and down all the way, like Innanna, into the deepest depths of the human psyche and there, at the root of it, we tweaked a few things.

"First we heightened women's pleasure in this world by causing gentle touching to trigger ovulation and hard handling to shut it down. Rapists and woman-beaters now fail to reproduce. Their kind is dying out, slowly, inexorably. Some women of our number are so sensitive to gentle touching that they conceive parthenogenetically. This has been a great boon to the lesbians and bisexuals among us. We have fewer children than our forests can feed, but every child is loved—not tossed into the dust to starve slowly or die of dirty water or be sold into sex slavery or the mines. As your children so often were. Until there were no more children to starve or sell.

"Later, we used horizontal gene transfer to shield women from the toxins of tickborne pathogens, mutated spirochetes, guided transposon shifts and microsurgical RNA transcriptions to defuse the ill effects of sex-typed myelin-phagic organelles. Incidentally, we cured cancer and the common cold as a side-effect.

"You are very young. You may not remember how quickly things changed when the tick-borne flesh-allergies became widespread. Hunters and survivalists holed up with their canned goods and ammo, perished first and in great numbers. You would be amazed how rich was their store of flesh and how poor their stocks of spirit. They treasured up bullets, burnt books and despised the weakness of their grandmothers. Soon they became no more a burden and a terror upon the land.

"Our sister clans of indigenes, far to the north and west, find their cabins by the number of wild boars who frequent their ruined dwellings. Our folk touch not the bones of the fallen, nor ease the throats of the swollen, thrashing bodies in their last throes of meat allergy. We bury the cans of spam in solemn ceremony to feed the ravening hunger of the blood-starved land.

"Now, the drone of mosquitoes in our surrounding swamps, the buzzing of bugs in the thawing bogs: these are as the music of martial drums to us, our defenders and our protectors. Rifles, airguns, arrows, blowpipes, all these we have left behind. Our happiness is secured by the whines of insectkind: their needle-nosed numbers and their biochemically exact zeronationing of our enemies.

"And the world, as you know, got warmer and warmer and warmer. The permafrost thawed, releasing spores and spirochetes unknown to modern man—but now survivable by still more modern woman. With proper nutritional support, pleasurable sensations every hour, intense loving kindness and care, our women beat the odds six times out of ten. As other peoples decline, we increase.

"We have no more winter; we wear no clothes. Neither of wool nor cotton, nor the death of the mulberry moth have we any need. Only for dance and ceremony, praise and pleasure do we don these skirts of string, leaf, vines, and beads. Twenty-four strings of beads we give unto each baby born whole among us. That is in mockery of the Old Ones who gave exactly so much in exchange for the whole of this tree-clad land.

"There was a cost, of course. But on the whole, the loss of the ability to eat, digest, or process meat, dairy, wheat and several other common food products was, for us a trivial price to pay. And we had already paid it in advance. So, that is how we—the much-despised and oft-mocked few—we, the not so much meek, as patient and long-suffering—we, the vegans, inherited this earth.

"Would you like to walk through our garden? We call it Eden two-point-one. Come, sing with me as we go:

> *Not to kill, berate, nor beat,*
> *no sugar, no honey, no fish, no meat,*
> *no dairy, no soy, no corn, no wheat,*
> *not even harsh words spoken shall we eat.*

"Our clade or subspecies is provisionally designated as Homo sapiens fructophagian. Here you will find only those who are unfit for the world of your making: those who constantly complained of anemias, allergies to electro-magnetic pollution, synthetic fabrics, who suffered fibromyalgia, chronic depression, all the ills of the spirit that earned us the epithets so liberally bestowed by your fellow men: weakling, whiner, wimp, woman-hearted.

"Yet, here we are: alive and thriving and more fertile than they who beslimed us with their spittle, their scornful ejaculations of abuse.

"See how we live in this paradise? Fish leap in our streams, the salmon runs again redden the waters of the rivers of the north. Lambs graze and kids skip about in the meadows in spring, but they do not live in pens and folds and byres beside us. We fence them out of our forest, not in. In times of abundance, we heap the overplus of our trees into thanks-offerings for all the wild things to eat their fill. The tar flats capture men on horse. The methane clouds do in most airships. Meanwhile, around our boggy rings, trees once more fill the world as birds, in growing numbers, lavishly seed the land.

"Sexual pleasure is one of the sources of our joy. It elevates us far beyond the farthest reach of alcohol intoxication. Do not think of us as unsophisticated savages. We know what kind of world you come from. We still eat fermented foods in lean times and imbibe hard ciders for ceremonies. Before we gave up the eating of all grains, we used to drink rich dark brews. Now, few of us have any need of such stimulants. The leaf of our fiber plants gives us all the flights of inspiration Mater vouchsafes to us.

"We see much of the world though we go not into it. It cometh unto us—even as you have come. Music we have, and dance and poetry and song—much that was degraded into mere entertainment for bored murderers and eaters of animal flesh now feeds us in spirit beyond your comprehension.

"We have become gardeners of the Mater: she instructs and we obey. Her plants tell us where they wish to grow, what ills they are able to cure. Man before the floods has no idea of the extent of our knowledge. The spirits of the land rejoice once more as we dance their ways back into existence.

"Hearken to me, now, young man: There are three trees in the center of our little Canadian paradise. Surrounded by a broad band of waters infested with alligators and wolverine fish, the Isle is cultivated to hold but three kinds of tree.

"One, we call the tree of the Knowledge of Carnality. Should the need arise, in some far distant time, when our people need to eat meat again, the fruits of this tree will reverse our physiological adaptations. There may be an ice age or a worldwide nut-tree blight that forces us once more to live as your people do. We bring our young people here at the time of their puberty. They each have the choice to relinquish the ways of our people: the sensual thrills of massage, the joys of pure eating, the dances and the songs. But if they eat of the fruit of that tree then they are driven out, forever, to live among your kind.

"Should you eat of the fruit of that tree, it will poison you, amplifying your extant propensities to the point of pain and permanent misery. You will live, but you may prefer not to.

"The second tree is the one we call the Forgetting of the Knowledge of Good and Evil.

"Should you wish to join with us, it is from that tree that you must sup. It will take from you all that you now hold to be of value: your culture, your learning, even your Gods. It will erase your memories and alter your appetites. Your old life shall be forgotten as your body adapts to our diet. Engineered enzymes in the fruit will take over your biochemistry.

"The effect of the fruit is drastic and irreversible. Even your beard and manly form will change to become frail, hairless, and epicene, like us. Or rather, like our step-children, the gentle giants among us. As the composition of your testosterone alters, your baldness will be replaced by shaggy, dry, dull red hair, like theirs. You will be like them in other ways.

"The treatment smooths the folds of the neocortex, via de-differentiated nerve-cell modification. Long-term memory loss is permanent, but the short-term memory capacity partially revives after nine months of custodial care. However, you will never develop the transmissible extra fluting of the neo-cortex that enables us to distinguish plant scents and deadly disease signatures. You will never attain sensory equality with our adepts. Instead, you will become as a child of god among us, sharing our joys and living as we do. We will teach you and reshape your mind in our image.

"Third and last is the tree of Death; we eat of that tree only in extremity. Should you choose badly, or regret your first choice, that is also a tree from which you may choose.

"Now that you have forced your way into the heart of our Ingathering, we shall not suffer you to depart and reveal our presence to others like you.

"I, and Guilliuana, who risked her life to have physical contact with you on your arrival, and many others like us, are the defectives of our kind. Imperfect though we are, we make a virtue of our failings. We have constituted ourselves as the Guardians of this place. Not all of us are utterly opposed to the act of killing. But we do not kill unless there are clear and sufficient signs. We do not, cannot know all Her purposes. Perhaps Mater has brought you to us to improve our chances of survival, to improve our general stock. Perhaps She merely tests our resolve and our fitness as a people.

"Know this: we might have robbed you of any choice. We might have administered the Touch by pouring an extract into your ear whilst you slept. Guilliana forbade us to do so, acting as your foster mother. You owe her your life, as we owe our lives to our mothers. It is our custom never to gaze at any woman except our mothers, so that we will love them as much as they deserve to be loved. Many men have stumbled on this one prohibition. Many men we have killed for the crime of staring at the women they desired.

"You are not the first man to come here. Nor will you be the last. It has been foreseen.

"Some, like you, we have brought to the Isle of Decision. Others, less well-intentioned, we have bound and left here, suffering them to choose ignorantly from the fruits thereof, or to die of starvation. Naked, but unbound, of your own free will, you have come to the Isle, to choose your fate, even, if you prefer, to brave the waters and so feed the flesh-eaters therein. These wolverine fish are how we dispose of our dead. Do not try to eat them. Their blood runs with mercury compounds toxic to you.

"Even now, it is in my power to deceive you, or to feed you of whichever tree I choose for you without your knowledge or permission. But in honor of your courage that caused you to seek us out, the persistence which crowned your search with success, the patience that permitted you to endure social isolation, and your undoubted membership in the fellowship of scientists, we give you the choice: to die with your mind intact, a martyr to your religion; or to give up your old life and the outside world, or to suffer as an experimental subject, testing the power of our science against your will.

"Do not blame yourself or us for this curious end to the curious impulse that brought you here. For all knowledge comes at the sacrifice of something else, equally important. Here, we neither explore, expand, nor exploit. We ingest, instill, infold. We live quietly, but quiveringly alive.

"As for me, I am old beyond the count of your people's years. I am tired. I come to the Isle to seek the ultimate happiness. For you, whatever comes next, your old life is done.

"We are marooned upon this Isle. In a month, they will come back to feed my body to the fishes and to deal with you. If you like, before I eat of the Tree of

Peaceful Death I shall instruct you how to distinguish among the Trees. By their fruits ye shall know them. Even as we shall know you.

"What will you choose, young man? To become as One or as Nothing? To struggle to the last or to accept what grace we can give? May Mater guide you to Her chosen ends."

Something To Look Forward To

by Dylan Siebert

"This is going to be good," said Marta's uncle as the bus wheezed up to the station. It was just past dawn and they'd taken in the February sunrise from inside the wide-windowed station, sharing a basket of sweet potato fries. "Vegetables for breakfast—nothing like it," he'd said to her as they dug into the hot, spicy mess. At twenty-five, Marta was past rolling her eyes at her uncle's humour, but it was the same line he used at almost every meal.

They picked up their bags, nodded to the fry vendor, and bundled out into the cold with the dozen other passengers. Up close to the bus, the smell of hot cooking oil washed over them in the crisp air, mingled with the scent of other fumes best left undistinguished. The station boy stowed their heavier luggage while the driver took their tickets. "Kitchener, is it?" she said, hardly glancing up. "We should be there by mid-afternoon." They climbed the steep steps and found a place near the middle of the bus. Marta gave her uncle the window seat.

"This *is* good," he said, looking around with obvious pleasure. Connor Bly was old enough to be her great uncle, ten and twenty years senior to her parents, who had themselves got a late start establishing their modest nuclear family. Uncle Connor had spent most of his adult life working for the Conservation Authority near Tobermory, and his hair and beard were pure white. But as he gazed around now at the soft lines of the bus interior, the faces of their fellow travellers, and the streets of Wiarton sloping up and away from them, his eyes were those of a child.

"This brings back so many memories for me, Marta. I used to take this thing all the time, going up and down from the peninsula. You know, back when people still drove cars all over everywhere and only us young folk took the bus." He winked. "Fifty-odd years ago it was an awful trip—you had to travel all the way over to Barrie and down to Toronto just to get anywhere, then stand around in the Bay Street terminal breathing in the smoke of twenty coaches, not to mention the murk of the city itself. But I loved it. There's such a sense of adventure to be had when the road is taken out of your hands. And of course, after all these years I get to say that I moved away from the city before it was cool." That last phrase had a meaning for people of Uncle Connor's generation that Marta had never been able to decode.

The bus certainly was different from the fifteen-seat vans she was used to. Those had been a constant in her life ever since her first summer working as a farmhand in Grey County. Even mid-season you could always find a crew with a van going south for cheap on holiday weekends. The bus, though, was spacious and comfortable, with ample opportunity for watching the countryside, one's fellow passengers, or just sitting quietly with one's thoughts. She watched as an older woman sat down in the seat ahead of her, her grey dreadlocks worked into a prim knot at the back of her neck.

"What are you thinking about, Marta?" asked her uncle. "So silent and serious! How do you like the coach so far?"

"It's pretty fine. I'm just thinking I could have used an egg in that breakfast."

"You get so spoiled on the farm. You've been finding fresh eggs even in town this winter, haven't you? Here, drink some kombucha, it'll help fill you up. Good for your gut too, after all that grease."

"Ugh, Uncle, you can keep your grandpa juice to yourself," she needled good-naturedly. "No one I know under sixty drinks that stuff."

"All right, I will," he said with mock stiffness. "Although when you get to be my age I think you'll take a much greater interest in your digestion."

"I'll stick with my cider vinegar, thanks. Keeps my head clear and my stomach settled."

"Did you say kombucha?" asked the woman with the dreadlocks, turning in her seat to face them. "So few people appreciate a fine culture these days, don't you find?" And she and Uncle Connor were off, reminiscing about good old times and bad old times and times so old neither of them could possibly have been alive to experience them. Marta's uncle had been a bachelor all his life, but he had never lost his interest or his flair for flirting. She tuned out as the door hissed shut and the driver piped up from the front of the bus.

"Ladies and gentlemen, welcome to Whippet Lines, this is the eight o'clock service to Owen Sound, Durham, Mount Forest, Arthur, and Kitchener, with stops in between. Got chickens or children, keep 'em civil or they go overboard. Bathroom's at the back, my name's Alice." The engine revved and Wiarton Station pulled away behind them.

"Hey Alice, can you throw my fiancée overboard? She's driving me crazy!" hollered a voice from the back of the bus.

"If I had a nickel for every time I heard that one I'd be driving a nicer rig than this, lemme tell you," called Alice. "I can help you out—but only if I get to keep the ring."

The banter went back and forth a while longer, the driver handling her hecklers with the ease and relish of a stand-up comedian. Snow-covered fields rolled into view as the bus hit the highway and accelerated up to fifty kilometres an hour. They passed buggies, big trundling wagons, and the occasional cargo bike, getting friendly waves from some as the bus pulled carefully around them. Marta's ears picked up the trail of her companion's conversation again.

". . . like my niece here. I always say, being single is a fine way to go, but if you want to do something else then you've got to get a move on. Were you ever married yourself?"

"Almost," smiled the grey-haired woman. "But we were so young, and things didn't seem so hopeful then. That would have been around the time we lost the war."

"You don't say! We could have been schoolmates. Now let me see . . ."

It was a useful handle for a certain period in the lives of people their age, since no one agreed on when exactly the war had been lost. It was simply a marker for the end of one era and the beginning of another. "Things had to get a lot worse before we could see how to make them better," Uncle Connor was fond of saying. But so many of his stories were about how crazy life had been before Marta was born that she took them with a grain of salt.

Satisfied that the conversation had steered safely away from her love life, she watched as the outskirts of Owen Sound began to flash past, each yard crowded with stakes and wire hoops poking through the snow. Then there was an ugly stretch where breakup crews had been working on an old big-box site. Some of the derelict malls around here were still producing good-quality steel beams and asphalt slabs after all these years. Marta had worked on a breakup crew one winter and it had reminded her of being a kid, sneaking into abandoned mansions with her friends just to rip stuff up. She hadn't enjoyed the work particularly, and had been glad when spring came to get back to planting and growing things.

There was a sizeable crowd at the Owen Sound station by the harbour, and the bus filled right up. The last to board were two middle-aged couples, one Old Order and the other New Order, their outfits identical save for the buttons on one pair of coats and the hooks and eyelets on the other. They were clearly dismayed to find that the only seats left were across the aisle from each other, in the priority seating zone just behind the driver. They sat down stiffly and ignored each other.

It wasn't just that one group was devoutly Christian and the other all back-to-the-land atheists, Uncle Connor had explained to her once. It was that each robbed the other of its uniqueness. "Why don't they just change their uniforms?" Marta had asked at the time. Her uncle shrugged. "Special people are all alike. It takes coming down to the milieu to be able to work out new ways of thinking." Coming as it did from a man who lived by himself out in the woods, that remark had surprised her, even if she'd known already how little he cared for either group. Old Connor had more gods crawling out of his left ear than any of them had in their whole universe, or so he claimed. She'd watched him summon owls out of the dark forest with soft, deep calls often enough to believe that her uncle was in touch with unseen powers of some kind.

At Chatsworth the woman with the dreadlocks was among the half-dozen who disembarked, and a young woman with Down's Syndrome took the aisle seat across from Marta. As the bus pulled away she peered past the Bly's to wave energetically at a grey-haired couple on the platform, who leaned against each other as they waved back. Marta complimented the young woman on the squash-blossom embroidery on her hijab, which matched the deep yellows and greens of her own scarf. They traded knock-knock jokes while Uncle Connor fell asleep, and Marta was able to practice some of the rudimentary Arabic she'd picked up on the farm. She couldn't have asked for a more patient conversation partner. But the best was when the man in the far window seat pulled out a cell phone and started talking loudly to someone who wasn't there, tilting his solar charger against the window at various angles. At that point the young woman turned to look at him and said, just as loudly, "YOU'RE RUDE." The phone conversation ended quickly.

Marta's new friend disembarked at Durham, and Marta decided to use the twenty-minute refueling break to stretch her legs. This was an important crossroads town, and the bus station was positioned just up the street from the impressive brick-and-glass building that housed the year-round Durham Farmers' Market. She followed the flow of Saturday shoppers down the street, and while a vendor just inside the double doors cooked her order of frybread, Marta scanned the crowded marketplace.

All that small-town Ontario had to offer was on sale here, and more. There were the winter staples of potatoes, carrots, beets, squashes, yams, daikon, celeriac, rutabaga, onions, garlic, turnips, and microgreens of every description, along with cheeses, milk, yoghurt, eggs of duck, chicken, and quail, frozen meats and cold cuts of bison through to guinea pig, jams, pickles, kimchi and other preserves, but also shawls, rugs, and shalwar kameezes woven in Europe, antique electronics and bits of small circuitry bundled in from California, soapstone and whale bone carved in the far North, herbal tinctures bottled in Brazil, salts of varying hues and compositions harvested from seashores and mountaintops around the globe, and souvenirs of Durham, Ontario, including but not limited to mugs, keychains, wallets, letter openers, penny whistles, pocket protectors, chopsticks, pennants, and paperweights. In one corner a brewer was displaying local honey mead alongside expensive American imports. Near the far wall a mechanic was demonstrating the action of a hand-built washing machine to a young couple and their snotty toddlers, the big drum whirring quietly as she pumped the handle. Just to Marta's right was an information booth advertising the local fuel co-op, and the beadwork on the moccasins worn by the man behind the table was so similar to that of the woman cooking frybread on the other side of the entrance that Marta wondered if their relationship went deeper than the obvious business interests they had in common. The only items she couldn't see for sale no matter how she craned and strained were sunglasses.

She paid for her frybread and hurried back to the bus. Uncle Connor lifted an eyelid long enough to wonder archly when someone would get around to inventing traveller's fare that wasn't desecrated in oil, but Marta ignored him as she tucked into the hot, fragrant food. A young man was coming down the aisle with a grey goose under one arm and a pack slung over the other shoulder. He was dark-skinned with close-cropped hair, and as he settled into the vacant seat across the aisle from her, she noticed that he handled the bird as if it were royalty.

"That's a fine animal," she said when she had finished her frybread and the bus had started rolling.

"None like her," he said proudly, stroking the goose's muzzled beak. "I'm bringing her for my parents in Kitchener."

"Oh really? I'm headed there to see my folks too. Are yours downtown?"

"Charles Street—you know the tailor shop across from the parkade gardens? That's us."

"No kidding. I grew up on Mill Street." The bus gathered speed, and Durham fell away behind them. The sun had climbed over the morning's overcast, and the winter fields stretched bright and vast on either side of the highway.

The goose stirred and muttered to itself. The young man smoothed the grey feathers slowly, patiently. "What do you do up north?" he asked, looking across the aisle at Marta.

"I'm crew manager on a farm outside Wiarton."

"Sounds like good work. Have to deal with a lot of town kids on your crew?"

She smiled. "Yeah, getting them to tell dogvine from runner beans is the hardest part. After that, backbreaking labour is no sweat."

He laughed—an easy, gentle sound. "You in it for the cash, or do you want to be boss some day?"

She'd heard that one before. Everyone had to decide sooner or later, and though she didn't talk about it often, Marta had made up her mind long ago. "I'd love to get land of my own. If they keep on shrinking the minimum acreage requirements I'll be able to afford it, too. My parents put me through Guelph Ag School stitching boots, and they'll back me for what they're worth. But I pick up work through the winter, and that's a bigger help. Drywalling, mostly." She was surprised to hear herself talk so much. Her dreams, like anybody's, were touchy things, and usually kept close to her heart.

The young man was nodding, smiling. "You must be the shining star of your family. Have any brothers or sisters?"

"One—an older brother. But he's crazy about computers, and that's been hard on our parents. They don't see a stable career coming out of it."

"What's he doing now?"

"Studying in the States. You can still get a full ride for that kind of thing south of the border. Weird country. What about you? What do you do?"

"Ever heard of Nickel Family Fun Farm?"

Her face broke into a grin. "Yes! I used to love going there on school trips."

"I help run the kids' programs," he said, returning her grin. He had perfect teeth. "Can I tell you a secret?" he asked, glancing around conspiratorially. She leaned in. "This is the goose that lays the phosphorus eggs."

Marta laid a hand across her mouth in feigned dismay. "The one and only?"

"Actually, they retire her every few years and replace her with a younger bird. Shocking, isn't it? I took part of my pay in kind this season. So old Golden Grey here will go down on my tax return, and Ma will have a good laying beast, and later on the feathers, too." He bent his neck toward the blinking animal. "Shh, don't worry. You've got a good long life ahead of you before feather bed time."

Marta smiled. "That reminds me of a song I heard once. 'Go tell Aunt Rhodie . . .'"

"Are you a musician?"

"I am. There's six of us renting together this winter, and we have a pretty good house band, if I do say so. Guitar, trumpet, tabla, I'm on banjo, Dolores sings. Hans only plays the spoons, but he's getting pretty sly with them."

"What kind of stuff do you play? Any particular genre?"

"Oh, Hot Soup, mostly."

"At the risk of sounding like a connoisseur, does your Hot Soup tend more toward the bluegrass or the Cuban Roots flavour?"

"Cuban. Alejandro's third-generation, and his parents sent him to Havana for a few years to be classically trained. His horn usually leads the band."

"Do you play any Sliced Bread covers?"

"Of course! They're the greatest thing since fried na'an."

"I heard them play in Detroit. People are always comparing them to Rolling Stone Soup, but I think their sound is way more original."

They talked like that a while, and Marta lost track of the towns rolling past. Suddenly she noticed they were in Waterloo, and that Uncle Connor was sitting up, awake and unusually quiet.

"Care to introduce me to your friend, Marta?"

She looked back to the young man, realizing she'd forgotten to ask his name.

"Faizal," he said, reaching to shake her hand and then Uncle Connor's. Marta completed the introductions, and Connor made the usual unclish inquiries.

"Nickels' Fun Farm, eh? That's near Chatsworth, isn't it? Ever spend time over at Kinghurst Nature Preserve?"

"All the time," said Faizal. "That forest is about the most awe-inspiring place I've ever set foot in."

"You're telling me! The size of those hemlocks . . ." Uncle Connor gesticulated soundlessly, his face rapt. "And all because those two Krug brothers had the foresight a hundred years ago to set aside the land from their timber reserves, with our enjoyment in mind. I've got all Krug furniture at my place and it stands the test of time, let me tell you."

The bus pulled up to Victoria Street Station in Kitchener, and there were Marta's parents on the platform, looking a little greyer and a little more childish in their anticipation than she remembered from the last time she'd been in town.

"There, wasn't that fun?" Uncle Connor asked as she reached for their overhead baggage. "One of these days they'll get around to putting in a decent rail service too like they're always promising, and that will be better. Faizal, good to meet you. Maybe we'll see you if we ever get back to Nickels'."

"Actually, my contract ends in April. I've signed on for the summer crew at a market garden near Hepworth."

Marta's ears tingled. "Hepworth! Which one?"

"Shady Acres. Do you know it?"

"Sure I do! It's just down the road from Sala'am Organics, where I work."

Faizal smiled that perfect smile. "Maybe we'll see more of each other, Marta Bly. That'd be something to look forward to."

And that was that. As she embraced her parents and turned to wave goodbye to her new friend, Marta thought to herself that he was right. And she didn't need Uncle Connor's elbow in her ribs to know it.

THE OLD MAN'S ASSISTANT PLAYS GO

BY WYLIE HARRIS

IN THE MORNINGS HE WOKE WITH THE TASTE OF METAL in his mouth. With his dreams of flight sifting away into whatever realms hosted them during his waking hours, he'd savor the precious seconds of peace 'til the shrill cries of the lieutenant's kata scattered them. Swaying in his hammock, gazing up at the row of immense bamboo rings taking shape in the space above their bunks, gleaming faintly through the storm of dust motes that raged slowly through the dim grey dawns. Higher still, the gaunt timber ribs of the hangar's roof arched in a warped mirroring of the bamboo skeleton's rowed curves.

Then the sounds of the lieutenant's exertions would unleash the mutterings and stirrings of a dozen dozen soldiers shedding their night's wraps. He'd heave a sigh, wrestle his twisted leg over the hammock's edge, and shuffle toward the old man's quarters in the warren of paper-walled cells against the rear doors, seeking his first duty of the newborn day.

His daily path into that flimsy labyrinth took him past the lieutenant's door, above which hung an amber-washed image of eight massive blimps not quite filling the hangar itself. No ribs to them—just shaped bags of air. Yet they'd a trick to them, the lieutenant said, a trick no modern balloon could own—with the wind cooperating, they could go where their captains willed.

"Old man's assistant!" called the lieutenant brightly from within. "You will attend me later for Go?"

"It is my honor, my lieutenant."

"Very good! Carry on!"

‡‡

The twin hangars' entire complement were cripples—survivors of downed balloons, returned to the nest to stitch and varnish silk and wicker to carry aloft some as yet still whole member of that elite brethren.

No such honor accrued to his own invalid status. The Big Wave had plucked him as a youth from his family's fields. The same root ball that he'd ridden to safety had betrayed him at landfall, twisting to put the tiniest of its twining giant appendages between his right leg and the sky. The old man had come floating down from the sky and hacked him free from where he lay pinned. Just that once, only freshly a cripple, had he known flight, seen as the birds. Since then he'd shuffled over earth only, and never seen his family nor their fields again.

More nights than not he flew again, as his dreaded dreams retold that tale, warped as was their wont. Through the sky, not the deluge, he rode the giant log, but it was weighted, sinking. Its roots twined round his feet, his ankles, and then the wooden behemoth rolled its bulk, ponderously, dragging him toward the crags and crowns of the landscape drifting by beneath and threatening there to scrape off or crush him against that seeming serenity—

His daily duties consisted in following the old man's whims. Here and there, those might hound him stumbling and crutching for a day or three amongst the toppled trunks of the giants that ringed the valley, to seek in the coolest crannies for the herbs the old man used for his teas. In the main, though, those minor and scattered whims receded in obeisance to a solitary great one. The ringed ribs above the bunks of Hangar Two were nothing less than the skeleton of a powered balloon.

Those ribs. He'd hung them, every one, through the long months of the clammy winter, rain drumming lavishly on the other side of the hangar's wooden skin. He might never walk again with ease, but going up a rope his ruined leg was no impediment, and his arms and shoulders had thickened implausibly through the endless ascents to the timbered arches. "Silkworm," the workers in their files below had named him.

But the worms that had spun the silk of old were gone from all but tales, and he thought of himself less as worm than spider. From spiders only, after all, did modern silk come, harvested patiently in its thimblefuls from pits a horror to all but their minders. Like a spider, too, did he move about the rafters, for once aloft he'd a virtual web of rigging through which to position himself for the latest stages in manifesting the old man's dream.

To call the old man hermit would have been a masterwork of tact. He laid eyes on that crumpled leather face oftener than anyone else in the hangars' entire complement—and at that such encounters but rarely came twice in a month's span. The mess stewards left his meals outside the paper door and reclaimed the leavings afterwards. His own instructions came oftenest as notes on onionskin. Where detail must be amplified, an occasional sketch sufficed, or a rare and delicate model—of paper, silk scraps, twists of grass. Components essential to his next task he would find laid out assembled upon the stained and ancient concrete of the corridor floor.

In any other command it might have been countenanced, or, more likely, expected, that such grand whimsy be never so much as considered, far the less consistently indulged. It might be attributed to the eccentric enthusiasms of the lieutenant, which seemed to rival the old man's in intensity and indeed to surpass them in their sheer variety. Yet the old man had pursued the solitary great whim under multiple commanders, many of whom had come and gone ere ever the spider arrived. As far as anyone's memory stretched, not one had ever been less than supportive, though resources were scant enough to render even the most vigorous support something meager in practice. Yet still the old man chipped away, like a prisoner digging to freedom with a spoonful of dust a day, the spoon the boy—the silkworm—the spider.

"How was it in your family's fields, old man's assistant?"

"In what way, my lieutenant?" He'd eventually decided the lieutenant's midgame conversational gambits were only that, no ploy aimed to distract. Even if subterfuge it were, it was wholly unnecessary. In all their time since the lieutenant first made him a captive opponent, he'd never come close to beating the officer. Why would he not seek some more challenging adversary? He supposed only because the spider alone in the hangars' whole complement stood apart from the military chain of command.

"Is it the same crop, in the same field, year after year?"

"Some do try that. They give their richest ground to the most valuable crop, season after season. But most hold that such practice exhausts the soil and invites disease."

"So. It is rice one year, beans the next?"

"Yes. Then millet, or sorghum. Yams, perhaps."

"But the same farm will plant the same area of each crop each year? Only in different fields from the one before?"

"I suppose so. Yes. Or nearly so."

"Such an intricate dance, throughout the seasons and across the land's broad face!"

He reflected that his family's share of the land's broad face would have fit within the hangar with room to spare—but said only, "Mm. Just so."

"Just so!" murmured the lieutenant, pushing his shining spectacles once more up his glistening nose.

‡‡

For generations their forebears had warred against the pale and wide-eyed hordes to the east, progressing all but imperceptibly from coastal toeholds to valley strongholds to fastnesses in the snowy peaks that now marked the empire's eastern limits. Yet in the aftermath of the Big Wave, when each village up and down the length of that ravaged land found itself an empire unto itself, for better or (usually) worse, what aid finally came was borne not on galleys from the home islands, but on balloons crossing the coast range from the colonies of the rich valley to the east. After that, the tax rolls went westward across the waves at first grudgingly, then sporadically, and lately not at all. Thus it was that of the balloonists who'd skied in any recent crop of dawns, the majority rode aloft not amongst the forbidding eastern snow crags, but rather over the rocks and spume of the coast, squinting for the first telltale wave tracks that would herald the arrival of a reclaiming, revenging fleet.

Coast or crags, war or uneasy truce, the lot of the Balloon Observer Officer was ever the same. Every young strong body lifted into the dawn might return burnt or maimed or lifeless, or might be whipped away into some hidden corner of the skies from which there was never any corporeal return at all. Those wracked but whole enough to live would be sifted back into the hunched rows in the hangars, stitching and twining and shellacking the vessels of similar fates for their successors.

Through that span of weeks the solitary great whim caused him to spend his hours aloft in his own share of lashing, uniting the rings of ribs with longitudinal members that ran the length of the borning craft. The shape it sketched under the hangar's arched roof was that of a dolphin arrested in mid-leap emerging from a mirror-still sea—narrowed to a point at the ends, muscularly plump amidships, with a suggestion of sleekness throughout for all that it was as yet only bones.

"Sergeant, your game is completed? I may borrow your board? Most excellent!" said the lieutenant smoothly, claiming his prize before the victim could begin to formulate a protest already foredoomed by the laws of rank. He laid the confiscated board beside their own, swept it free of stones.

"Imagine this grid populated with beings," he said, indicating their own gameboard. "The cells of your body, if you like. Trees in a forest. Precisely what sort is of no importance.

"What matters is only: surrounded by less than two, or more than three, living beings, the central being must die." He placed a black stone in the first intersection of the confiscated board.

"Elsewise, it lives—or, if dead, regains life." He placed a white stone upon the next square. In the same fashion, he continued to examine each square of their played board in turn, then place the proper stone in the corresponding square of the appropriated one. After several rows, he paused. "You see?

"It is the Conway variation!" the lieutenant announced, rummaging in his satchel for a thick bundle of onionskins, which he laid out smooth beside the twinned boards. As he lifted the pages and began to riffle through them, back to front, the spider could see that each contained a sketch of an enormous Go board. As the pages blurred, one into the next, strange fishlike formations emerged, floundered awkwardly across the grid, and vanished. "The Game of Life."

Transfixed, he reached for the pages to repeat the riffle. Remembering only too late that he must ask permission, he stiffened, but the lieutenant waved him eagerly on. "You see? In stasis, change. In change, stasis. You see?"

He was squinting against sundown's last reflected glare at the image of those eight balloons contained within the hangar's vastness when the lieutenant approached from behind.

"The problem is not the wind itself—but its strength relative to that of the balloonist. In the old days," the lieutenant gestured at the photo above his door, "there were powerful engines that ran on fuels bled from the very earth. Those veins run dry; those engines rust. Many of the engines fall, flake by flake, into the acid baths to make the gas that inflates the balloons. We have now only," he said, giving the spider's shoulder a squeeze, "our own muscles to oppose it. On a calm day we can do wonders. In a barely stiff breeze we run before it at our peril, even as in the balloons. In a gale—we long for the impossible return to our mothers' wombs!"

Whence the skin came he'd no idea—every hand's span of silk was prized. But during the days when he made the final ties between ribs and rays the scraps began to accumulate on the floor below, the pile of pale silk—not quite gray, nor yet pale blue—slightly larger at each evening's descent than when he'd heaved on the line in the dawnlight.

The day he began to put the skin on he despaired of ever finishing. The bamboo members of the skeleton had a rigidity that had allowed him to fix them in place, however many painstaking transits up and down the length of the craft the serial adjustments required. The silk slipped and twisted and refused to be held tight or made fast.

Toward the middle of the third such fruitless day a persistent and unfamiliar tremor in his web distracted him from his near-tearful frustrations. After a time the vibration ceased, just as the familiar pair of gleaming spectacles appeared at the top of the ascent rope. White-knuckled, the lieutenant fixed his gaze on the underbelly of the balloon's skin less than a meter from his perspiring face, and there paused wheezing for a period far longer than it seemed the climb would extort from one accustomed to his fanatical regime of calisthenics. At last he swiveled his head toward the spider. "I am to be the old man's assistant's assistant!" he proclaimed.

The old adage proved as trusty as ever; with two of them laboring within the spider's web, the silken skin spread enwrapped the bamboo skeleton with an ease and speed he could never have achieved alone. From there they progressed to rigging, control linkages, lead lines—all the surreptitious minutiae of the old man's draftsmanship. Each day below them a brace or two of wagons trundled in from the railhead with sheets of new silk and salvaged rags; each day a pair or more left bearing a gondola carefully packed with the empty envelope that would fill and carry it and its pilot into the air.

"Truly it is amazing, my lieutenant," said the spider in a rest break on one among those days, as the other poured tea from a vacuum flask. The stream of clear brown liquid wobbled, threatening to trespass beyond the bounds of the cup's rim. The lieutenant's brow knitted above the spectacles' twin moons, a bead of sweat releasing itself from the tip of his nose to thread the web and stretch itself toward the hangar floor far below. "The old man's ability to hold all the intricate pieces of the design in his mind."

"Truly spoken, old man's assistant!" the lieutenant gasped between clenched teeth. "Perhaps more so than you know!"

"How so, my lieutenant?"

"Well!" the lieutenant replied, whuffing out each phrase between controlled breaths, like the cries of his morning kata. "As you have perceived, the old man has the admirable ability to hold the design in his mind, at once entire! What I suspect you may have yet to appreciate is this: he can, as well—and even more importantly—envision the sequence in which each piece must be added to achieve a working whole."

"I see, my lieutenant," said the spider, in dubious tones.

"The fields of your family's farm, old man's assistant! How did you choose which field to plant with which crop?"

"We did not so much as choose, my lieutenant. The crop to be planted in a particular field, we knew from what that field had grown in the season past."

"But did no one ever choose, old man's assistant? Was it like the riddle of the egg and the chicken?"

The spider reflected. "I suppose the only choosing would have been when my grandparents' parents first assumed their tenancy. From that time forward we but followed the pattern they set then."

"Just so! Your forebears' choices set a pattern which you followed these several generations hence! As in our games of Go! Do you not at times wish, as the game nears its conclusion, that you might have chosen one of your earliest moves differently?"

"Indeed, my lieutenant. It is often so. More often than I would wish it. But surely the old man's ancestors built no powered balloons for him to learn from? And he cannot have learned the art of it from any games of Go!"

"Again you speak truly, old man's assistant! Yet we should not attribute too godlike an intelligence to the old man. His mastery, like any such, has its roots in past attempts—not all of which have been successful. Indeed, one such created the opportunity for me to rise to the command I now hold!" He smiled faintly, wryly. Briefly. Heaved his chest upward to draw the air within.

From dangling corners of the netting flung across the balloon's skin they hung the drivetrain, a narrow tubework of bamboo with a thin loop of metal chain down its narrow throat. From the fore end, like a dragonfly's head, protruded a gearbox with a set of pedal cranks to either side. He thought the old man's self-schooled engineering must have failed him—nowhere was the space between the cranks and the balloon's skin adequate to permit a pilot to sit upright.

After a long moment hanging still in his harness, twisting slowly amongst the dustmotes, he became aware of the spectacles' gleam upon him.

"You pause in your work, old man's assistant! You have some misgiving?"

"No misgiving, my lieutenant—only misunderstanding. The need for two pilots I understand—to drive the craft with greater force. But I see no way for them to sit in order to pedal."

"You see well, old man's assistant! You need only apply your thought to what you see. The pilots lie prone and pedal with their hands!"

"Thank you, my lieutenant. Now I see."

"It seems there may be more yet for you to see and think, old man's assistant. This design has a special implication for you!"

"Your pardon, my lieutenant. I do not see it," he said, hope rising improbably, unwilled, like gas from the depths of the bogs without.

"Surely you suspect, old man's assistant! But let me dispel the anxiety of uncertain hope. None in this facility has more strength of arm and body than you. You have been the builder of the old man's dream. Now, you are to be its engine!

"Hold!" he cried, as though to cut off a response the spider had yet to snare from his spinning mind. "In such situations the forms must be observed!" From his tunic pocket he extracted a flattened roll of onionskin, tied with a narrow wisp of tattered silk and wax-sealed with an officer's signet. "Congratulations, old man's assistant! You are the first Civilian Observer Auxiliary in the history of our corps!"

On the eve of their maiden flight the lieutenant summoned him for their regular game. "It is natural to think of altering the routine to mark such a momentous occasion, old man's assistant. But on the other hand a such a disruption can upset the nerves. For just such reasons do soldiers drill so endlessly.

"So!" he continued, producing from under the table a bottle of rice wine. "We plot the middle course. We will play our game as though this were only another night in Hangar Two. Yet to celebrate our achievement, and the promise of the morrow, we will accompany it with an unaccustomed treat!"

Some number of cups later, the spider began to feel that his behavior towards the lieutenant had perhaps been too reserved. The officer clearly felt fondly toward him—and after all, he had no formal military rank nor role. A sudden fear struck him: what if, rather than offending by over-familiarity, he rather gave slight to the lieutenant by maintaining a too formal demeanor?

Thus emboldened: "My lieutenant, I have a curiosity. The old man—how came he to this place? These pursuits? I would ask of my own, but . . . he is not unkind to me, but neither is he the least open. That is—toward me he behaves the same now as on the day he brought me here. His face is carved as of wood."

The spectacles threw back the lamplight's glow in a long moment's regard.

"It's said he was the greatest of them all," the lieutenant said. "Balloon after balloon wrecked under him. Always he displayed the most courage! Always he emerged unscathed! Never did his nerve break!

"Finally the command removed him from the duty roster. It was thought that his death or crippling in action would be too great a blow to morale. That the observer corps benefited from living proof that one among them might survive to a hale old age."

"My lieutenant—this old man?"

"Our very own!" the lieutenant beamed. "My commander's commander heard it directly from the former chief of corps. Yet when the big wave came, he disobeyed orders. He was the first aloft! He saved many lives. This you have witnessed for yourself. I was not so very much younger than you are now, at the time, old man's assistant. His fame after the rescues was legend. Yet after that his status was even more complicated. The role model on his pedestal must not disobey! So he came to be here among the cripples. None may go against him even if any willed it—yet never may he depart."

"Your pardon, my lieutenant—the greatest of them all?"

"So I said, old man's assistant. My own path to these hangars I trod through shame, not glory. I failed Balloon Observer Officer training in the first free-balloon exercise. Afraid of heights! Now I am a coward sent to rule amongst cripples."

The gleaming spectacles disappeared as the lieutenant's head tucked. Hastily the spider stood, rattling the board. "I yield, my lieutenant!" he blurted, and fled the paper maze.

He scarcely slept that night. The alien whooshing of the bellows hurrying the gas upward through its tubeworks from the acid vats, the steady sprinkling of the rust flakes to their fizzling doom, as the bag was filled. These sounds kept him awake far into the night and filled his dreams with strange visions.

On the morrow it was as if that final night's game had never occurred. Only the throbbing behind his eyeballs remained as evidence. Side by side before the assembled ranks of cripples they donned their caps, their scarves. Their goggles. The spider ascended first, and squirmed from the tail forward to grip his pedal cranks. After him, the lieutenant—the reason for his sweating and panting now painfully plain. The spider was thankful his post afforded him no way to twist back and watch the lieutenant as he squirmed forward. He marveled at the man's formidable self-mastery.

The tremble that ran through the craft's body as the towlines took hold from below was most unsettling—a structure fixed for all its existence suddenly come loose from its moorings, following different forces along a new axis. To a sustained cheering from the towing troops below, the nose crept—slowly, liquidly—past the arch of the hangar. He caught a glimpse of the old man's wizened, upturned face, improbably small. He heard a strangled gasp from the lieutenant—turned to see the spectacles oriented steadfastly horizonward.

"Old man's assistant! Let us fly!"

Taking his cue, the spider reached back to grasp and yank a toggle by his waist. The wickerwork hammock pressed against his belly, and the loosed ends of the guylines coiled earthward.

After some immeasurable span the pressure on his vitals eased. The lieutenant checked a dial strapped to his wrist. "Two hundred ten meters and neutral buoyancy!" he announced. "Let us apply power!"

As one they bent themselves to turn the cranks before them, on which they'd scarcely loosed their grips since first squirming into their flight stations. The gossamer fans aft responded quickly, surely, to their mechanical urging, and the craft itself surged forward. His sphincter tightened at a sudden roar to forward, and the marsh itself seemed for a moment to rise up to meet them, but it was only the marsh fowl rising from under the menace of the craft's shadow.

After a ten-count the lieutenant released his cranks and felt for a smaller set of burnished metal grips below them, manipulating them with the greatest care. They swung right, then left. The craft's nose, with them slung below and aft, went through a gentle counterclockwise corkscrew. From the lieutenant, a cackle of amazement.

"The fear is gone, old man's assistant!" he cried. "It was no fear of heights, nor of falling! Only—of the loss of control!" With that, he swung the nose coastward and reapplied himself to the cranks with rapturous abandon.

The spider advanced his cadence to match the lieutenant's. Already his shoulders and upper arms were beginning to ache from the unaccustomed motion, the awkward position. He shifted in his rigid hammock, wondering how long it would take blisters to rise on his chest and belly. In his dreams he rode the log in the silent, effortless glide he half-recalled from his rescue by the old man those years ago, the start of his life in the hangars. Now he saw again as a bird, as in that memory, but there was this clackering. This exertion.

The lieutenant ran them westward as far as the last range of hills between marsh and coast, then swung them in a broad arc south, then west, and finally back northward along the seaward edge of the higher inland range, sketching a hangar-centered orbit around the rim of its bowl of marsh.

"Look!" the lieutenant cried, nearly catching a finger in the works as he abandoned cadence in the urgency of his gesticulation. "There's the scar from the fire six years ago. Covered in alder saplings. All around it, Douglas fir, alike to what grew before the fire where the scar is now. Come back in ten years, or a hundred. There will be a burn scar somewhere, about as big, full of alder, and with about the same amount of Douglas fir surrounding it. For the firs in the burn, it is the end of their centuries of life—a catastrophe! For the others, it is nothing. For the alder—a rare stroke of opportunity! For the landscape, it is only the normal course of life."

They landed even greater heroes than they'd been upon going aloft, to a fresh rush of panic from the marsh fowl and another rousing tide of cheers from the hangar cripples. Two more flights they made in as many weeks on the brightest and stillest of days that stretch of spring could offer, so clear that they could shoot bearings on the snowy cones of the interior peaks.

Not till the fourth flight did the lieutenant fail to veer them into their lazy circuit of the hangar's marsh, giving the craft instead its head to ease on slowly toward the gap in the low line of hills that separated the hangars' marsh from the rocky coast. Ahead of them the coast's eternal haze of spray rose up toward a tattered ceiling of grey cloud.

As they threaded the gap the craft yawed about gently, shifting its nose slightly northward. The lieutenant frowned as he readjusted the guidance levers. They yawed north, south, back north again, in a lazy spiral. "A breeze stirring abaft," he muttered. "Probably only funneled by the hills."

They rose a bit. In the near distance to the north they saw one of the balloon shore pickets. Far to the south the spider imagined he could make out the shape of the next down the line, a ghost lurking in the trickery of the constant damp grey.

The spider realized their cadence had slackened. "A pause, my lieutenant?" At the bob of the spectacles, he reached back to rub each shoulder in turn. Their forward motion continued. It was not so quick as a trot, nor yet perhaps as slow as a walk. Certainly speedier than the spider's terrestrial shuffling.

Pedals stilled, they spied to the south one of the longshore pickets to the southwest, its balloon aloft and canted westward of the tether boat. Awaiting the turn in the wind to make its run back shoreward. The lieutenant heeled the nose around to the southeast, and with no word passed between them, they as one applied themselves once again to the cranks. Yet as the slow moments passed in wretched contrast to their frantic cadence, it became clear that their nearest approach to the tether boat would occur somewhat to seaward of it.

The lieutenant ceased pedaling once more, breath coming in rapid shallow gasps, so different from the deep, controlled heaves of his kata. "As the balloon waits for the wind's shift," he said, "so shall we, old man's apprentice!" He resumed his hands' sluggish communion with the control levers, coaxed the nose again into its slow leeward spiral.

The spider wore no timepiece and had no nerve to query the lieutenant as to how much time had passed since the coast lost itself in the mists behind them when the first of the black hulls hove into view to the west. White sails lashed, regular in their spacing, oars flaying steadily at station-keeping. The lieutenant's gasping switched in a heart's beat to a wheeze. "Invasion fleet!" he rasped, as his hands allowed the nose to begin the ponderous swing that would point it again into the wind. "Pedal!"

So for the first time they dared assay their strength directly against the wind's, knowing beyond fear what the outcome must be. The crackling of the shipboard troops' weaponry preceded only by moments the deep thunder of the ships' own ordnance, and far too short a time later they began to hear a curious pattering, as of raindrops, against the balloon's skin. Scattered splintering cracks against the shellacked bamboo of the undercarriage. A line parted, throwing the spider five centimeters toward the lieutenant's hammock by his side before banging up painfully against the ribbing of his own.

The lieutenant consulted his wrist pieces. He sought to orient the nose to leeward once more. The spider needed no such contrivance to register their descent toward the waves, to the invading fleet's ships. The flapping rush from the balloon's flayed wrapping above left no doubt in any case.

Without waiting for the lieutenant's cue, the spider again applied himself with furor to the cranks. After a dozen revolutions the spectacles swiveled to behold him; after another score the officer's hands went numbly to his own set. The lieutenant hissed in what might have been triumph as they cleared the bare mastworks of the nearest troopship by bare meters, but the spider felt him dragging at the cranks, slowing him even as he strove to further hasten the cadence.

They were skimming the wavetops now, careening over the curving lines of foam at a crazy angle, every fiber from his fingertips to the base of his spine afire. The first wave to touch them caught the nose and flipped them, sickeningly, up over the tattered skin of the balloon. The balloon slammed back down on its back like a slain whale and they rode for a time like that, bellies bare to the grey sky. He remembered his passage over the floodwaters, aboard the rootball, a lifetime before.

Then he was squirming backwards to aft through his wicker cocoon, conscious as he floundered that the lieutenant was motionless at his station, whether dead or merely stunned he knew not. No sooner was he free than he dragged himself back up the exterior of the lieutenant's tube. He saw no outward sign of injury—could hear, at that proximity, the rapid, rasping gasps. "My lieutenant!" he shrieked, and shrieked again, but the officer did not so much as turn. With a roar he smashed both fists against the wicker caging, but even splintered by shot their work was true and would not yield against his pounding.

Frantic, he lunged at the flailing end of a parted line and threaded it through the lattice to make a loop fast around the lieutenant's ankles. With a too-familiar twist, the balloon shrugged the gondola a quarter-turn deepward toward his right. He ran as much slack as the line would give into the tubeway and then dragged himself aft to the entrance, shoving himself backwards into and through it 'til his hale foot rammed the lieutenant's. He fumbled up the end of the line, looped it round his shoulders, and threw himself into a series of savage pulls. He'd almost cleared the tube again when the craft gave its final settle, plunging him into the burning cold sea. The loop of line around his shoulder sawed at the cords in his neck, pulling him under. He flailed himself wildly free of it and fought back to the surface, grabbing handfuls of silk like ladder holds to wrench himself gasping back into the air. His eyes cleared the stinging spray to show him a second line of black hulls to westward.

"I yield, my lieutenant," he murmured, and gulped desperately for air as the shattered craft rolled him once more toward the numbing waves.

ROOT AND BRANCH

BY CATHERINE MCGUIRE

I PUSHED BACK THE LAST OF THE SHUTTERS. The sun was finally topping Hawthorne Hill, splaying light through the schoolroom windows, across five round tables ringed with small chairs, a half-circle table on one wall holding precious art supplies, and up front, the chalkstone wall, the low shelves of books, paper and pens . . . and my desk. My first real Mentor's desk. Not exactly mine—none of this was *mine*, but as much as a mentor could own something. In the back, to the right of the door, the small iron woodstove waited for winter. On the other side of the door, a small treadmill to run the overhead fan was tucked behind a graceful indigo tarp used for outdoor exercises. Unlike the schools where I'd apprenticed, this room had a clear glass roof panel to maximize natural light. It also had four brass oil sconces evenly spaced between windows, two on each wall. It was a well-made, attractive room. And from first through fifth days for this school season, it was in my care.

Soon the children would be arriving, but this moment was a chance to pause, breathe my thanks to the cosmos and to walk slowly around, checking that everything was in place, harmonious for the start of this day. "Each day precious, each day a gift," I murmured as I straightened the student slates and charsticks, welcoming the children in my heart. After my long journey and first lonely days, something in me was settling as I repeated the routine.

In another moment, I heard their voices as they climbed the gravel path—Dale always the loudest, laughing at some bird and trying to imitate its song; Juda singing in her high-pitched six-year-old voice; Lern hollering back to his younger brother Omer to "hurry up!" Laughter and chattering became a song weaving through the shrubbery, joining with the birds' dawn chorus. After two weeks, I was beginning to know them, learning what worked best to open each child's mind and heart. I stood in the doorway with open arms, smiling. When they saw me, the twenty children called out and capered up into the play yard, where they formed the morning circle. After the summer deluge season, school was still new enough that everyone was excited. Putting their lunch sacks at their feet, they held hands and waited.

"Bless you all and bless this day, bless our minds and what we say," I sang as I slowly paced around the circle. "Nature give the light we need, we the soil and her the seed." The children repeated the song twice, Ki's tiny sparrow piping soft next to twelve-year-old Jared's husky tenor. I noted that Dale was wriggly; I'd have to find him a physical task today.

"Welcome children, let us begin." I led them into the schoolroom, by now well lit by morning sun.

Juda paused at the door and looked up.

"Please, Mentor Elia—my Mum asks if you would like to come to dinner next waxing third?" The girl's brown eyes sparkled.

"Tell your mother I would be very pleased to come by," I replied with a smile. Juda practically skipped to her chair. It would be a change from the journeymun meals; I hoped the mother was a good cook.

The children organized themselves at the tables by level—the first subject was always writing, with some older children side-by-side with the sprouts, as family jobs kept them from practicing or attending. But there was no shame; they knew they would be regrouping later in other subjects, and each child's level was unique.

"Thank you, Omer, for bringing the lesson." Ki broke the silence, but gratitude was always an allowable interruption.

I smiled at the little redheaded, bark-hued five-year-old I'd nicknamed "Ladybug." Ki was doing it more to get approval, and at her age, that was normal. My challenge would be to teach her real gratitude. I patted her on the shoulder quietly, refraining from praising her to the class, vowing to find a moment today when Ki was authentically grateful, and use that. Instead, I repeated the girl's thanks, allowing Omer his proper acknowledgment. The boy blushed deeply, a rosy glow on bronzed cheeks. Having their printed example, all settled down to practice on their slates. I wandered the tables, correcting and praising, noting improvements that might shift a child to the next table level.

All was quiet until a sudden "Ow!" burst out of Dale. Everyone looked up, and he scowled and pointed at Lern. "He kicked me on purpose!"

"Dale—what do we know about making assumptions?" I said as I strolled toward the table. The other children looked down at their lessons, but I knew they were listening intently.

Dale frowned and opened his mouth as if to protest, but caught himself, took a deep breath, and replied, "We don't make 'sumptions. We ask." He tugged at his chestnut curls in mute frustration, his green eyes wide and staring. At my nod, he continued: "Lern, did you kick me on purpose?"

It was obvious from Lern's anguished look, but with young boys, the lesson had to be enacted in full to have effect.

"I didn't!"

I was now at the table, with a hand on each shoulder. "So, Dale, Lern says he didn't. We believe people unless there's reason not to, so what do we do when there is an accident?"

"We forgive and let it go," Dale mumbled, looking down.

He didn't look quite willing to let it go, so I prompted, "Remember Clawfoot and Whiskers?

> Snarly Clawfoot, mad, sad and feared.
> No one, no one, no one came near.
> But Whiskers was brave and clever. He saw
> limping Clawfoot, tugged the thorn from her paw.
> Clawfoot said sorry and kind Whiskers cheered.

"You can be like Clawfoot or Whiskers. *You* make that choice."

I could see his inner struggle as I patted his shoulder. I'd heard that his family was having difficulties, but knew no more than that. After a moment, a smile reached his face and he said, "I want to be Whiskers." He held out his hand and Lern shook it, and they once again settled down to copy the names of local herbs.

When the sun reached the top of the bookshelf, I instructed them to switch tables for reading. Juda retrieved the five books from the shelf, histories written at various levels. The others squirmed and whispered; I'd learned this was their favorite—the time of storytelling and getting to ask questions about mysteries that puzzled even their parents. I always started with the older students. By the time the young ones' attention began to flag, it would be their turn to read.

Jared stood and began where they'd left off yesterday. "Many lands had become empty once the contagion had passed." He stumbled over *contagion* but kept going. "Gradually, the native plant and animal life returned, except for those areas where damage from toxin or where"—he looked up imploringly and I walked over, whispered the word—"*industrialization* had created dead zones. Balance slowly returned, and after many generations, humans returned also. This time we were careful to consider the needs of all life, to learn the cycles of season and lifespan, and to respect the limits the Mother Goddess had set for this area." Sagging with relief, he passed the book to the blonde girl on his left and sat.

She continued: "Honoring the mysteries beyond our com . . . pre . . . hension, we committed to learn what was ours to learn. The healing habits of plants and minerals, the tek . . . neeks that provided food without destroying ha . . . bi . . . tat, and the customs that allowed us to live in harmony. Never again would we fight over possessions, facts, or whose God was more important."

If only that were true, I thought, but made no comment. Best they learned the ideal first. It was said one of the unbalances of ancient times was piling too much into a young mind. I gestured to the next table and the mid-level students read another couple paragraphs on what was known of ancient civilization. But it really was a background—the lesson was about compassion and balance, about how a responsible adult lived in the world. For this basic schooling, before they became apprentices, I taught the four Cs: communication, compassion, creativity, conduct. Other details they picked up as they grew and lived in their town, as much or as little as they needed.

It was down to the sprouts' table now, and Ki was stumbling over the story of the poisoned well: ". . . and they all had to move and leave their town behind, because one mean person spoiled it," she concluded emphatically.

I peered over her shoulder. "It doesn't say 'mean' there, does it, Ki? It says 'selfish.' It says 'destroyed,' not 'spoiled.' Read what is there."

"It's the same thing!" the child protested.

"Not exactly. 'Selfish' means you are thinking only about yourself and not others. 'Mean' suggests an intent to harm. People can be self-centered yet not *plan* to hurt others."

Raising a cautious hand, Lern asked, "In my section, it said they fought over fact and holy mystery—but why was that a fight?"

I repressed a frown. This was still mostly guesswork. "As far as we can tell, some had become very possessive of the facts, as if facts were *theirs*, and others felt the same about the mystery of life and spirit. Because their sense of ownership of everything was so strong, it leaked over to things no one could own, and so they fought as if they might lose their possessions. It sounds strange, I know, but ownership was perhaps their main pride."

"But—no one can own an idea, or . . . a tree or . . . or the Spirit!" Jared's expression flowed from confusion to frustration to disgust.

"*We* know that. It seems so sensible now. But elders have learned that once people did indeed try to own ideas, and they actually fought when two people claimed the same idea. They had gatherings to judge whose idea it was."

There was a ripple of laughter from the class—the youngest laughed because the others did, but even nine-year-old Dale seemed to picture and reject the notion. Jared shook his head slowly.

"It sounds like they deserved to fail," he said.

"No one *deserves* to fail, not when all the facts are known," I replied. "We must have compassion for them no matter what harm they did, because they were doing their best with the ideas that they had. Amerka, just like the Meyans, and the Romings and the Giptians, fell apart because they lost their balance, lost even the *value* of balance, and thought that more was better in everything."

"More brings less," Juda said solemnly.

"Mistakes are a chance to learn," intoned Omer.

"Yes, thank you Juda and Omer. Now we understand cycles of abundance and decline, and the process of trying and learning from mistakes," I replied.

"Thank you Juda and Omer," Ki piped up.

I bit my lip to keep from smiling. "And speaking of learning, shall we go outside and check the weather?"

The students eagerly filed outside, the older ones pairing with the younger to examine clouds, determine the direction of breeze, check the opening and closing of the various plants in the garden, and to check the homemade tin-and-leather pressure gauge that gave some warning of change. Dale was cavorting from plant to plant, and raced over to check the pressure even if it wasn't his turn—but he needed to run. I gave them a few minutes study, then clapped my hands and they returned to form a circle.

"What have you learned?" I asked them.

Their answers were exuberant and fanciful, and the discussion went astray into whether plants could think, and if clouds could see what would they see? These were good chances to discover what each child found interesting. One of my tasks was to help the Council consider what apprenticeships they would have at thirteen. And like plants, children usually gave early signs of what place they had in the world. In respect for nature's wisdom, I was to help each child blossom.

It was late afternoon before I finished my notes and cleaned up, then shuttered the windows. This was half fifth, so school would be out until waning first. After turning the key in the stubborn wooden lock, I brushed the chalk dust from my marigold-dyed tunic and pushed my unruly bark brown curls back behind my ears. Once again I noted with amusement that I almost matched the new cedar clapboards. I was more at home here, where skin tones ranged from peach to night-black, than in the last town, where most folks were pale and blonde. But it was the same struggle getting to know the adults here; a stranger had no accepted place. So unlike with children. Giving myself a shake, I set off down the path into town, a half-mile away.

Like the other three towns I'd lived in, Aurora was nestled beside a river that fed the town with trout and provided the fastest route to their trading neighbors. In late afternoon, many apprentices trudged with delivery carts, parents romped with children in yards and I could hear shouts from the bank of the river. The bathing pool must be crowded today. As I walked toward the main square, I feasted my eyes on small cob and stucco homes, vibrant herb gardens and shade trees casting fantastic shadows on fences and water barrels. One house had a porch on three sides, and the spindle pillars were decorated with blue, green and gold ropes wound in a striped effect. I imagined myself living on this lane, gently closing my curtains at evening. Another yard had delicate wind chimes of carved shell; the music followed me down the street. Half consciously, I composed a few sketches for the next time I had a moment to draw.

With eight hundred residents, Aurora was slightly smaller than the two towns where I had apprenticed, but it had a full slate of industries and shops: blacksmith, printer, glassworks, grain mill, biofuel plant, spinners and weavers, baker and grocer. This town even had a butcher, though it was a small shop. The previous two towns were vegetarian, and I was glad of the change; I had been brought up with lamb and chicken. There were dozens of small traders at the weekly market—the sweet maker, toymaker, hatter, wood turner, the farms that brought vegetables, honey, eggs and fruit. I loved to browse the stalls, although my position only paid with room, board and a very small barter chit. I'd met a wonderful seamstress and a wood turner whose elegant wooden pens with brass nibs would set me back three mooncycles of barter. And there I first was introduced to Rameda, a gray-haired woman full of smiles and plumpness, one of the town elders—in fact one of the two leaders they called "Beloved."

The town's main square had a Council Hall, message/transport office, a small museum with salvaged artifacts, the Peacekeeper's office with cells for disruptives and—my destination—a two-room library where some ancient manuscripts were housed alongside the newer books and sheets of news from other areas. I spent at least three evenings a week there, devouring anything I had not yet read.

I paused in the doorway, watching Marl reading at his usual table, the second of four arranged crosswise in the long narrow room lined with shelves. He was a thin, slightly stooped young man about my age, with large sad eyes, unruly black hair and long shapely hands constantly darkened by the inks and glues needed for the books he was learning to bind. I hadn't counted on Marl. I'd come here on my master teacher's recommendation, planning to grow my skills and experience in a place that respected scholarship, until I could qualify for a job in Mastersburg, the capital, which had the biggest library anyone knew about. I would be friendly and helpful here, contributing to the community and hopefully bringing with me several written recommendations when I moved on. But after a mooncycle in this town, other feelings had surfaced.

I would have been interested in chatting even if Marl had looked like a frog, because books were my passion, but he was attractive in a quiet way, and we quickly fell into the habit of dinner after the library closed on fifth days. Since neither of us had yet achieved Mastery, we ate for free at the journeymun housing where I had a room. Marl lived with the printer/bookbinder, getting away when his duties were complete.

I tapped him gently on the shoulder, but he still jumped as if under attack.

"I'm sorry, Marl," I murmured. "I didn't mean to disturb."

"No matter. I was finishing. Are you hungry?"

I actually would have preferred a little time to browse the books, but I nodded and he gathered his box of old manuscripts, handing it in at the main desk as they left.

Marl was as silent as Ki was talkative, so he didn't ask about my day, and I had learned to wait until we were eating to inquire about his. So I enjoyed the soft breeze on my face, the easy gait as we strolled down Second Street toward the journeymun hostel where I lived. The line for the meal was less than a dozen—I hadn't realize I was so late.

"Hope they have enough left," Marl commented. He seemed forever hungry; his fear puzzled me.

The dining room was noisy and cheerful, with nearly thirty journeymun who for various reasons didn't eat at their masters' homes. We walked past long board tables each seating a dozen. I heard chatter about the upcoming potlatch, to coincide with harvest celebration. I worried about that—I didn't have much to give away, and would be embarrassed to receive more than I gave. It was past time for me to do a few sketches of the area and people, so that I could gift.

When we finally reached the buffet, we found plenty of red bean stew, squash with honey butter, bread, and a kale salad, then located a table in a quieter corner. Mostly couples used this table. Though we weren't "a couple," I liked to chat undisturbed and the other tables were generally group discussions.

"Last time you were telling me about the botany book that the Explorers Guild commissioned," I prompted.

Marl shrugged and swallowed before speaking. "We're almost done gilding the frontispiece—goes on display at the capital library after Day of Balance. Cover's calf leather, dyed woad blue. Calf took ill; wasn't sacrificed."

"Good to not waste, but not destroy," I murmured, trying to picture the volume. "Is it bound over cord, to give that spine pattern—" I gestured, trying to describe the look of ancient tomes.

"Yes, much like that. Makes it sturdy. The title is lettered in oak gall ink on spine and cover."

"They used to add the author's name," I commented, picturing Darwin's *Of The Species.*

Marl laughed. "Yeah—back when that was important. Writer's name is on the frontispiece, but not the cover."

Out of the corner of my eye, I noticed couples holding hands, or leaning close to whisper and giggle. *They probably wonder what we're doing, just chatting, stuffing ourselves.* At twenty-two, finished with my apprenticeship, I was older than most here and should be at least considering if I was going to take a partner or choose a solitary life. Since mentors didn't own their schools, my lifepath was slightly different, but it was just as tricky to find a partner with a compatible career. For example, farmers and teachers rarely got together. Likewise, researchers who were uncovering scraps from ancient civilizations partnered with other researchers or botanists and lived a nomadic life. Tradesmen and shopkeepers usually met at area fairs, the established partner taking in the newer one, or both going to a town needing that skill. After partnership, people didn't generally move around, unless there was a break in the relationship, which was a grievous thing for the community. So choosing a partner was also choosing a community.

But even after meeting a number of hard-working and capable young men, I hadn't felt the urge to settle. Did I have the *wanderlust* that had doomed at least two cousins to a life of poverty and odd jobs? It gnawed at me. Focusing on training was all well and good, but I was expected to also be planted somewhere. "A tree cannot grow in air," as the saying went. This was the first time I'd even considered a partnership, and I saw no sign that Marl was thinking the same way. He lapsed into silence after dinner, helping to take down the tables. As usual, we walked along the river for a short way then joined the evening taychee in the square.

Because I had to be at school before dawn, I had to miss the town's morning meditation, but I tried at least twice a week to attend the evening session. The slow, graceful gestures of taychee, done in unison in the central square, created a meditative flow that pushed out leftover niggles—I'd found that old word and loved it—so that I could move on from the day and be present for evening. It was also cheering to see everyone from little old ladies to seven-year-olds try to match their gestures to the whole. And it was a link to my birth town—the same gestures, the same slow melding of breath and body—making the universal flow visible as it was in plants and in weather.

Today I was distracted by awareness of Marl beside me, his awkward movements, his frown of concentration that surely blocked flow of harmonious energy. He looked like he was fighting with an invisible demon. I reminded myself to focus on my own flow, and to do my part to create group harmony.

When the session was over, Marl nodded to me, saying "Okay, until waning fifth, then." He turned and walked toward his lodgings and all the harmony I had managed to create drained through my feet in a single gush of grief. *What was wrong??* Was I imagining a connection where there was none? Perhaps this was just a way for him to pass the time. And until this evening, that's what I told *myself* it was. But this grief said otherwise. And now what? I went to sleep that night aching with my first real bout of homesickness.

‡‡

The sixth and seventh days of every week were spent differently—the sixth was community service, and the seventh was given to gratitude and meditation, to re-grounding and realigning with the universal energy. Some made offerings to Nature, or the Goddess of Mercy, some honored their ancestors, but as little daily work as possible was done, to balance activity with rest. New sevenths were the large celebrations, and full, waxing, and waning sevenths were individual observances.

As an outsider, I was often recruited to help clean or repair various town build-ings, but this sixth I'd been asked to join a conflict resolution meeting as Witness. Usually it was older townsfolk who did this, so I was puzzled and excited—did they want my mentor skills? I was met at the Council door by Geralt and Lil Banft, who'd sat on my discernment committee, when the town had checked to see if my compassion and skills warranted accepting me as mentor.

"Greetings, Elia. Thank you for helping us with Dara and Assed's meeting," Geralt said.

So it was Dale's parents who were being brought in for guidance! My task was suddenly clear. I would be asked to speak about any effects on Dale and his two sis-ters that I might have noticed. Quashing my hesitation, I nodded and smiled at the Banfts, found my seat, and searched my memory, trying hard to weed out uncon-scious assumptions.

The meeting began by ushering Dale's parents to the two facing seats in the center, almost touching, so that it would be difficult for the Ryo-Gans to ignore each other. Dara was tall, thin, with bushy walnut-hued hair, her eyes the same jade green as Dale's, her skin a slightly paler cream. Assed was darker and a head shorter than his partner, broad shouldered and be-whiskered, with long chestnut hair tied in a tail at the neck. He was continuously scowling, hunched in his chair.

"Dara and Assed, dear members of our community, you have been quarreling in public over the last mooncycle," Geralt began. "We grieve for your unhappiness, and have asked you to come here so that we may help put it to rest one way or the other, for the health of our community." Geralt gestured at each one, holding cupped palms as if giving invisible balm to each. "Since you have been here before, we will only touch on the guidelines before we start. We ask that you look at each other the whole time, refrain from raising your voice, name-calling, accusations without facts, and that you be open to the testimony of the witnesses and the guid-ance of the elders. Do you assent?"

They nodded, Dara with more eagerness. Not that they really had a choice—if they refused this Council, they would have to leave town and it wasn't easy finding a town to take a family without references. I felt a sudden panic—I didn't want to lose Dale, who was a delightful child despite being as active as a flea.

"Then let us begin," Lil said. "I witnessed the two of you shouting at each other last waxing fourth, standing in the market. As I remember, Assed, you said that Dara was deficient in her performance of her role as mother and partner—I will not use the same hurtful words—and you threatened physical harm—"

"I never threatened to hurt her!" Assed interrupted, turning to look at the circle.

"Please keep your gaze on your partner, and allow the witnesses to speak without interruption." Geralt's voice was quiet but firm, and the man mumbled apology and turned back to face Dara, who was struggling to appear calm though her shoulders were shaking.

"I also overheard an argument last waning second, in which you, Dara, stood at the door of the blacksmith's shop, calling out to your partner, asking him to come home with you, but also calling him shaming names in front of at least a dozen of his friends."

Dara hung her head briefly, and said nothing.

The meeting preceded like this for a half hour, with four witnesses describing public incidents of anger and argument. My heart sank as I waited my turn—if it had leaked out into the public this much, how bad must it be at home, where the children would overhear harsh language and maybe even threats? Would they even allow this couple to continue in the same house? I had heard of mandated divorce. How bad did it have to be before the elders removed children or separated the partners? I searched Dara and Assed's faces for any hint that they realized how serious this was, but their frowns looked like nine-year-olds'.

"And now Elia, our new mentor, would you describe what you have noticed of the behavior and emotions of the children, Dale, Su, and Waali?"

I gathered my thoughts. "My first observation is that Dale is continuously over-energetic, often unable to keep his seat or focus on his lessons without interacting with other children. Even allowing him to run the fan treadmill doesn't seem to lessen his wriggly behavior. And sometimes he races on it to cause a wind, as if he enjoys annoying others. And he is very quick to take offense, where the other children don't seem to be. The younger two are much quieter, in fact it is difficult to get Su to talk or read out loud. She seems more withdrawn than other children. However, I hasten to add that I have only been teaching them for a little more than a mooncycle and I don't know if any of these behaviors are rooted in the child's nature." I glanced over at the couple—Dara looked triumphant; Assed was scowling.

"Before Council gives their guidance, do either of you have anything to share with us, remembering to follow the guidelines of this meeting?" Geralt asked.

Assed raised his hand first so Geralt pointed at him.

"I've been . . . much irked by . . . having to carry more of the burden of this partnership." Clearly he struggled to find words within the guidelines and that expressed the anger that suffused his face. "My position at the bio-fuel plant flattens me, and she . . . that is never taken into account. Plus I have an hour here and there to enjoy with my friends, and she . . . these are constantly interrupted with so-called emergencies. I ask the Council to explain to my partner what equality of burden means." He glared at Dara and sat stiffly with his fists clenched.

Dara tried to look at him, bit her lip and looked over his shoulder—technically permissible but not really according to guidelines. "I think there are many in town who could attest to my willingly carrying my part of the burden in this partnership. In public, I have not raised my voice until Assed did, and I tried not to respond, but how do I defend myself against this level of anger? We have three children who are suffering from our difficulties, and I can't make that right by myself. I ask the Council to mandate conflict management classes for my partner, so that we can continue to parent our children."

"Thank you, and I appreciate you both for following the guidelines. Would you please step outside now?" Geralt asked.

Once the couple had left, the council was silent for a long moment. I had expected to be excused, with my part over, but I wasn't, so I watched and listened eagerly—I might be assigned to such a Council later in life. The discussion brought up other meetings and other incidents that went back several years, and watching their grim expressions, I wasn't surprised when Geralt summed it up: "I believe we have given them every chance to commit to harmony above individual desires. At the very least, I believe that children should be moved to another house. And what I've seen today does not give me confidence, so I would suggest we also split the couple and ask that they not meet or talk for at least six mooncycles, with council members assigned to help them parent separately. They should each meet with selected guides, to see if they can own their part in these disagreements and identify ways to act differently. Does anyone have a different conclusion?"

No one did, so they called the couple back and gave their decision. Both Dara and Assed were shocked, despite so many incidents—they both started protesting at the same time, but were waved to silence by Geralt.

"You know you don't have to accept this guidance, but if you do not, you will be asked to leave Aurora by the end of this mooncycle. We act for the harmony of our town, and we believe there have been sufficient attempts to change this in other ways. You do not have to decide today—you can tell us by tomorrow. However, we will be watching your family and will act to prevent any conflict, any risk of injury to either you or the children until you give us your answer."

"I accept your guidance," Dara said quickly, "and I ask that myself and my children be protected immediately."

"I *don't* accept! I don't want to break up our family! Dara—" he turned to her with his hand out, but she turned toward the Council.

"It is only for six mooncycles," she said, not looking at him. "I would rather try something new—we haven't done it well on our own."

Several councilmun smiled; admission of failure was an excellent prognosis for change. But it took two for success.

"Given Dara's answer, we consider this partnership suspended," Lil said. "The children will be immediately taken in by the household of Rameda, to nurture them while you two focus on the possibility of harmony. Dara, you two left the children with Rameda, correct?"

Dara nodded. Assed seemed for a moment like he would challenge the decision, then he sagged and walked out of the room. After thanking the council, Dara left through another door.

Gerald thanked me, and asked that I take special care to help the three children as they adjusted. "We know the household of the Beloved is very warm and nurturing, and we will provide ample opportunity for the children to see their parents and to ask questions. But I would be surprised if they did not act differently until they have settled in to their new situation."

I assured him I would be very alert and that if questions or problems arose, I would ask for guidance. Even trained mentors were not encouraged to rely solely on themselves in difficult situations. "Many hands carry the burden better," I concluded, and he smiled.

As I heard the schoolchildren coming up the path on waning first morning, I was grateful I'd attended the meeting. Without that, even if Council had informed me, I'd have far less understanding of why the Ryo-Gan children were upset. I heard Dale's angry voice and the sound of wood hitting wood, and I hurried down the road. The other children had stepped away from him, huddled and staring; he was hitting an ash sapling with savagery, yelling, "Stupid, stupid tree! You tripped me!"

I took him by the shoulders, and eased the stick out of his hand.

"Children, go on up to the circle. I will be there soon."

Dale quivered in my grasp but didn't try to break away, and once the others had disappeared around the curve, he burst into tears and clutched my waist.

"Dale, dearheart, I am so very sorry that you have been hurt by your parents' separation." Even as I said the carefully rehearsed words, I knew they wouldn't work. I knelt down and hugged him tightly, letting him sob on my shoulder. Were there even words to help a child in such pain? I'd had two children lose parents to death, but this! Was this easier or harder—your parents across town but out of reach?

When the crying storm ended, I gave Dale a handkerchief to wipe his eyes, and told him it would be alright if he wanted to spend the morning alone at the art table, making pictures or reading.

He nodded, then burst out, "If I wasn't so loud, my da wouldn't be so angry!"

"You are a wonderful boy, and you have no blame in this," I said, lifting his chin so he looked at me. "Sometimes adults get confused just like children, and sometimes their confusion makes them angry. Your mom and dad are confused, but they have mentors now, too, and you have the Beloved to take care of you while your parents focus on their lessons. Come, now—"

I led him up the path to where the other children were waiting silently in the circle. Their faces showed that they knew the basic story, but I wondered how much they understood, with broken partnerships so rare. It was only then I realized Waali wasn't present. The Beloved must have kept her home. Su stood by her friend Juda, grasping the other girl's hand tightly and looking down. I hid my grief and smiled; I led them in the morning prayer before escorting them inside.

Dale hesitated, then walked to the art table and sat with his back to the class. I asked Omer to distribute the writing samples, and I took a small lump of pottery clay from its tin box and placed it before Dale. At first he just stared at it, then started poking, then pounding, flattening it with his fists. I glanced at the others—they were looking back and forth from their slates to Dale, but mostly focusing on writing. I watched the boy for a while, decided he needed a bigger lump of clay, and smiled in relief as I watched the double handful absorb his grief and rage and gradually calm him. He moved from pounding to sculpting some four-legged animal. *Nature provides such mysterious gifts*, I mused. Clay had helped me to cope with my mother's death. I was relieved to find it worked here.

Halfway through the morning, I realized Su was glancing longingly at the art table, so I excused her to join her brother, and the girl chose a charstick to doodle on a rough piece of paper. Seeing that, Dale switched to drawing, covering the page with wild sketches of houses on fire. But his mood was calmer, so I could focus on teaching the others. Still, it was a long day and I was tired when I released the children, then impulsively decided to escort them to town. I could tidy in the morning, and this would prevent any emotional outbreaks.

I knew it was a good choice as we got closer to town and Dale got quieter and quieter. I could guess where the family had lived by his hunched shoulders and quick glances down Grace Street, but he didn't lash out and I dropped the two children at Rameda's without incident. There was just time for a nap before dinner.

My second-floor room was big enough for a single bed, a six-drawer dresser, a writing table and armless chair, and a tiny wardrobe, but at least I didn't have to share it with another apprentice. I'd managed to squeeze a three-shelf bookcase by the bed, to hold the few volumes I owned and those I could borrow. There was a blue checked curtain on the window overlooking the slope to the river, where several vegetable plots still had colorful foliage. At dawn, I would wake to hear the grain mill, or the toot of some steamer going upriver. It was a peaceful, lovely room. On my wall, I'd hung my mother's and an uncle's exhibition embroidery samplers, and a landscape watercolor by a student who'd cried when I left. I had little else—my denim travel bag, three outfits for school and one long tunic for dances and ceremonies. My sister's hair comb that fell from my hair too easily—give that in the next potlatch; no point in holding onto it. Appreciate the gift and let it go.

Although the bed was an old straw tick on a roped frame, it felt wonderful to stretch out. I hadn't realized how tensely I'd held myself all day until I felt the shivers through my muscles. I began deep breathing relaxation, releasing my fear and grief to the greater flow of nature, breathing in the quiet air and natural peace, as I had been taught. In a few minutes I slept, waking refreshed by the delicious odors of roasted squash rising from the eating hall below.

The chatter along the tables was about the separation; not surprising, but I felt tension return as I picked up my meal and sat beside the weavers' apprentices, Dell and Hannah. These young women—sixteen, sandy and ebony, both tall and slim with none of the hunching that eventually overtook weavers—were my favorite dinner companions when Marl wasn't with me. Today, they were gossiping in low voices while stuffing in food. I frowned and deliberately took a moment to give thanks, then raised my fork to my mouth slowly and with attention. The two girls took the hint, slowed down and treated the food with more respect, and I kicked myself for acting the mentor with adults. But they didn't stop gossiping.

" . . . and he was discovered drunk as a winter lightdancer in the straw at the stables!" Dell finished. She looked horrified but also curiously triumphant.

"Dara didn't come to work at the message center this morning, my sister said." Hannah's expression was more solemn, fearful.

I didn't want to gossip; I could feel the skewed energy of talking about someone behind their back. So I changed the subject.

"Can you tell me how the potlatch is structured in this town?"

For a moment neither girl answered, then Hannah said, "We bring everything to the town square and it's given away—what else?"

I paused. I'd picked the topic at random, and searched for a question. "Are there any restrictions on what can be brought? I mean, must they be useful items, or could decorative pieces be given?"

Dell nibbled a sweet roll thoughtfully, looking off in the distance. "I know that Lars the house painter once brought some decorated wooden signs that he offered to paint names on. Does that count?"

"What were you thinking of bringing?" Hannah asked.

I reddened. This wasn't a good topic. "I . . . I couldn't carry much from the last town, but I sometimes draw pictures. I don't know if—" I stopped and looked down. Did I sound like a have-nothing?

"Well . . ." Dell paused a long while before continuing, "I've never heard rules about the gifts, only that they be given freely." But the doubt in her voice told me enough. There were always unspoken rules, some not known until broken. The girls had grown up here; they learned by doing, as with most things. It was always "as nature intended." Until it wasn't.

"I will ask an elder," I said, and finished my meal in silence, grateful that they switched to chatting about the complicated patterns they were learning. I felt the pang of being a stranger, despite their consistent welcome. That was another part of the Time of Seed Sowing—the brief period of wandering to a new town, of discovering small differences and unspoken expectations. The lucky ones never left their hometown. But I'd have missed much if I'd been able to stay in Aspen Grove.

After evening taychee, Lil Banft came up and asked, "How are the children doing?" She guided me to a bench on the edge of the square.

"Dale was angry at first, but when I allowed him to work with pottery clay, his creative nature reappeared and he was calmed. His sister joined him at the art table and they both seemed relieved to draw out their feelings in pictures. I have seen that happen before. Waali wasn't at school, but she smiled from the porch when I delivered the older two to Rameda's."

"Young children often bounce back more quickly," Lil murmured, staring at her hands on her lap. She looked up. "I'm sorry that you have such a challenge so soon."

"Nature uses what is at hand," I quoted from the Book of Gratitude. "I am glad to be of assistance. I only hope—" I paused.

"Is there a problem?"

I shook my head. "Not with Dale or Su. I am just not sure how to respond if other children have questions or comments—there is such a thin line between wanting to help and making judgments. I want to guide them correctly."

Lil's smile was sad. "Yes, that's true for adults also. I might suggest to the children that they speak to their parents if they have questions, and that they practice attention and compassionate listening, rather than giving advice or opinions."

"That is a wise idea, thank you."

I paused, wanting and not wanting to ask Lil more about Marl. Was that gossip or asking advice?

"Is there anything else?" Lil was quietly attentive, showing no signs of impatience, but I faltered.

"I just . . . I just wondered how potlatches were arranged here."

By the time the waning fifth came around that week, I was bone tired and relieved at the break, happy to turn the children over to the care of their parents and the community. It had been a struggle to stay in the moment, to resist impatience or the confusion and worry that rippled through the class again and again. It had rippled through town as well, so who could blame the children for picking up on it? There was enough disturbance that the Beloveds had called a meeting for the waning sixth, to let townsfolk discuss their concerns and problems. I wasn't looking forward to it, though I was open to hearing any useful ideas. But before I attended that, there was this evening and Marl to deal with.

I stopped at the door of the library and watched him for a moment—did he seem more tense, or was my own worry coloring my gaze? This time he glanced up and noticed me, but startled in the same way. How could it be that he wasn't prepared for my coming? What was that fear? But I said nothing as we went to dinner, and even our conversation during the meal was muted, as he described how they finished the special book and packed it carefully for transport to the capital city. I longed to ask other questions, but it wasn't until we were seated at a bench along the riverbank that I finally worked up the courage.

"What . . . I mean, do you have plans after you finish with Master Rhogan?" I realized I was clenching my hands; I deliberately relaxed them.

Marl looked over my head, toward the trees, frowning. "There's enough work here, if I want to stay. But more work in the capital."

"Yes! That's where I want to go—eventually," I said, not wanting to seem grasping. "I have heard the library is the best anywhere. But I imagine many people want to work there." I suddenly felt light, joyous. Perhaps there wasn't a choice to be made—we could travel together! But that dark voice cut in—*has he shown any interest yet?* My next question died in my throat.

Marl was tracing a circle over and over in the dust of the bench. "I—I realize. What I mean to say is—we've seen each other a lot." He glanced up and immediately back down. I held my breath. "Gant the wood turner congratulated me yesterday—about us. You know." He glanced up and down again. "But—there's something you need to know."

"You prefer a male partner?" I knew I was blushing, grateful he refused to look at me. "I would understand—"

"Not that. No, I've wondered . . . could I even *be* a decent partner?" He paused, took a huge breath, continued. "You know I was orphaned? Not supposed t' be a problem—children always taken in. But—still a big hole inside." His words jolted out like stones falling down a slope. "Wasn't an easy time. Flu took so many. Went to four houses before my new parents survived." He stumbled to a halt. When he looked up, it was with the imploring glance I had seen so many times at school. *Help me out with this,* he was saying.

"I'm sorry to hear of your pain," I said, picking my words carefully, wanting to touch him but sensing his prickly energy. "I appreciate your honesty, and I sense in you a real compassion—*true heart*, as we say. I was blessed to have my parents until I was eighteen, and I have four aunts and uncles whose love also nurtured me. I see you are loved in this community, and I believe—I hope—that we are able to bloom despite starting in poor soil."

"I've hoped that. What if that's *wrong*?" His hands gripped his elbows like morning glory strangling a stalk. "What would I do t'you—to any partner—if I—if this hole inside won't heal?" His laugh rasped. "Town works so hard to find us a place. But even our Beloveds can't do magic."

My gut roiled. I thought of Assed—could childhood pain have caused his anger? Would Marl be like him? To get this close and to discover a partner was out of reach—that wasn't fair! I wouldn't accept it.

"We know that flowers don't bloom before their time, and that often the plant looks . . . sparse before then. Neither of us have to make an immediate decision. You have your books to make, and I have promised to nurture these children. Can't we wait and see what blooms?"

Marl covered his eyes with both hands. "Oh, yes—lovely metaphor! They never mention pain. Do flowers hurt as they grow? Does it *ache* to bloom? Even reaching out this far is so hard—please try to understand." He dropped his hands, looked away. I could see traces of tears. "Don't know if I could stand t'get closer, have it fall apart. Maybe better to be a solitary, do my job and not expect any more." Abruptly, he stood and walked away.

I fought for breath, feeling like I had been kicked in the stomach. *This couldn't be!* He was a gentle man, and meticulous in his work—so many wonderful traits. Why this blight? I watched him leave, his form growing fuzzy as my tears flowed.

The rest of that evening was a blur for me and I felt twice as heavy and slow as I joined the others the next noon. When I arrived, the square was filling, with people coming in from every street. They had created a stage for the Beloveds, and placed a half circle of benches for the elders; everyone else would stand. There was a lot more concern than I'd realized. The Beloveds had been attuned correctly. Instead of the usual chatter, people were quiet, with thoughtful expressions. Families seated their elder one at the front then walked to the open area in back. School children were allowed to sit at the feet of the elders so they could see. A tap of a cane on a shoulder quieted any unruly child. It was more solemn than a full seventh celebration. I didn't see Marl anywhere.

I stood between Hannah and Dell, searching the crowd—would Dara or Assed be here? I couldn't decide which would be worse—having to hear your neighbors speak or sitting home alone, wondering what they were saying. I was answered in a moment when Lil and Geralt arrived with Dale's parents. They sat in the elders' section, their backs to the crowd, sparing them—I thought—the need to control their expressions. And a moment later the Beloveds—Rameda and Lyle—stepped onto the low stage. I hadn't met Lyle—he was a tall thin man with a gray fringe of beard, a bald head the color of polished cedar, and a wide smile.

Rameda began, "Good friends and townsfolk, bless you for joining us to discuss what our town needs in a time of confusion and apprehension." She looked around and raised her hands as if to embrace the crowd. I stilled my impulse to look around, trying to ground myself and focus. "It has been more than a year since such a meeting, so I remind you that those who wish to speak must start off with our usual confession before asking a question or making a comment. And of course all questions or comments must come from the deepest, most compassionate part of our hearts, and be focused on the harmony of this town." She stepped back and Lyle stepped forward.

Confession?? I glanced around, but saw no confusion elsewhere.

"Good friends," Lyle began, his deep voice carrying easily over the crowd, "we are grieved at the pain of our friends Dara and Assed, and we are committed to helping them regain as much harmony as they will embrace. And we also commit to regaining the balance that may have been disturbed by any incidents of anger or cruelty. This is a time for us to make note of places where the balance has faltered, and suggest actions to assist in the town's healing. We ask that you keep your comments short for now, and longer discussions can be arranged later, as needed." He stepped back and gestured with both hands, as if welcoming a guest.

There was a pause, then a hefty, muscled man walked from the left side toward the stage. He was night-dark like young Juda and I wondered if he were related. He stepped on stage, but not to the center, first nodding to Dara and Assed, then directing his question outward while looking at the Beloveds.

"I, too, have been angry enough to punch a kinsmun," he began, "and I ask my friends, what can we do to calm an argument before it boils over? I myself pledge to speak calmly and avoid sharp words even when I think I am in the right." He bowed slightly to the Beloveds and left the stage.

A line had formed to the left of the stage, and now the baker, a thin woman who must be newly Mastered, stepped up. She repeated the first man's gestures, then said, "I have spoken harshly about others behind their backs many times, and I ask forgiveness. And I also ask, how can we learn from this without having our discussions turn into gossiping? I myself pledge to speak about my own experience, rather than presume to understand what happened in this situation." She also bowed slightly and left.

After three others spoke, I noticed a pattern and began to see why the "confession" was required, though it hadn't been so in other towns. Each person seemed to direct that piece to Dara and Assed, and although I couldn't see their expressions, I saw Dara nodding once or twice. It probably *would* be comforting to learn your anger or other flaws were shared. And the confession ensured that the speaker couldn't take a superior position. Each of the questions were good, reflecting concern about the town's harmony, though I couldn't understand how they'd be able to discuss all of them today.

As it turned out, they didn't even attempt it. Townsfolk continued to step on stage and ask questions that mostly carried their own answers, pointing out something that had gone wrong and pledging to change behavior, subtly encouraging others to do the same. Only one speaker, an elderly man who stamped his cane on the stage for emphasis, made any accusatory suggestion. He stated that, in his long experience, there were "some people" who were angry at the world and did not accept others' help in regaining harmony. "To them is the hardest road," he finished, and Rameda stepped forward, put her hand on the man's shoulder and guided him off the stage, returning and for the first time responding.

"There are words that are true on the surface," she observed, "but like the bramble with roots that burrow and invade unseen, also carry feelings that are only recognized when they have done damage. Our town is like our body—what damages one does harm to all. And like the branches of a tree, we are all connected whether we would or no. As our ancestors discovered, our world is too small to separate *us* from *them*. And I have found that looking in the mirror and recognizing where my frustration originates helps me every day."

I couldn't see the old man, but there was a small ripple of movement, suggesting he hadn't taken the rebuke well. In the crowd, which had been silent, a few murmurs drifted like bees buzzing. Beside me, Hannah commented, "Old man Argent should certainly know about *that* problem." She giggled and Dell reached around me and tapped her shoulder.

"Shhhh! Gossiping!" she whispered, but she also was smiling.

The meeting lasted from high noon to half-westering—there were many questions and suggestions, most of them were either about restraining anger or avoiding gossip and judgment. Even though nothing had been answered, I felt the tension ease in the people around me. Finally Lyle stepped to the front of the stage.

"Thank you, kind friends, for your participation and helpful suggestions. We have a hill to climb ahead, but what I hear makes me confident that we will re-ground and rebalance ourselves and reaffirm our commitment to harmony. And thank you Dara and Assed for your willingness to attend and listen. If any here believe we need deeper discussion on anything, please speak to me this first day when I am at the Council office. Good evening, my good friends and peace be on your houses."

The townsfolk scattered toward the various streets, still solemn but not as silent. I heard one matron tell her partner, "The sad part is, we can only improve our own behavior—that guarantees nothing."

"But it does contribute to our health, like we bolster our bodies with herbs even though we have not the ancients' medicines for flu," the other woman replied.

I avoided those I knew in town and headed for the river, to think about the meeting and my own crisis. Most towns I'd lived in had harmony councils, but never such a large group discussion. Certainly group meetings were needed for troubled acquaintances, bringing in those they would see every day and their families so the solution would work as widely as possible. But "life water sprinkled farther carries less healing." I would've guessed that such a large group would have done almost nothing, and yet I could feel the difference as people left the square. As if putting their concerns in a group basket, they were relieved of some personal conflict. Should I ask for a guidance meeting for me and Marl? But that was an individual problem, not affecting the town's harmony. Not yet.

Instead, I decided to try an empathy routine learned at school. Back at the room, lying down, I breathed deeply and focused my mind, slowly drawing back from the room around me, bringing my awareness to my heart center, grounding myself on the bed. Then I began the empathy meditation, one essential tool that all mentors practiced—putting oneself as deeply as possible into the feelings and attitudes of the selected person. This was so much harder when a loved one was at stake! I had thought myself skilled, but as I tried to touch the awareness of being a child without parents, shifted from home to home, too young to understand why, I kept seeing the adult Marl stooped over his books; I lost sight of the child.

Was my pain interfering? Was it survivor guilt? Sometimes the fortunate became defensive in the face of misfortune. Again I detached, focused on my breathing, and moved back slowly, remembering childhood sensibilities, and only then trying to add an orphan's pain. After a half hour, I pulled back to myself, not really successful but knowing that too much would unbalance me. After drinking water, I went to the desk and wrote a letter to my master mentor, some general questions about empathy, but also asking if I had any flaws that would prevent this connection.

‡‡

The next week at school was hard; I was constantly chastising myself and dragging my attention back to the children. Dale was subdued, not angry as before, perhaps finally moving into grief. Su was even more withdrawn, and I tried to find little jobs to bring her in contact with others without pushing her. Each night after school, I made a point of attending the evening meditation, trying to achieve the inner balance that eluded me.

And when new fifth came, I walked to the library with a tense gut. It wasn't exactly a surprise when I didn't find him, but I still walked back to the only book-shelves that could shield anyone, and only then, when it was clear Marl hadn't come to our meeting, did I give in to tears. Giving up on dinner, I headed for the river.

It was an overcast evening, as dreary as I felt. This Snake river was twice as wide as the one I grew up along, and the murmur of its current sounded like a strong wind. How different this walk looked when the sun was dazzling the swift water and flickering through the hazelnut and cherry trees! Then, the whole world looked excited, alive. Now the river sulked along the edge of town, and the trees stood indifferent. Not for the first time, I wondered if Nature experienced herself that way. Humans were very prone to telling stories, and yet why would they be given that instinct if they weren't supposed to use it?

I scuffed through dead leaves and looked for anything of beauty to sketch, that might lift my spirits. Of course he wouldn't come—he had told me his truth, and I needed to accept it. *Life moves on.* For a few minutes, I watched the great wheel of the grain mill as it caught then spilled the green-gray water with a grumbling hiss. The town was debating whether to build another wheel, to power a communal cooling house, something more reliable than a root cellar, as the winters were still getting warmer. It would need a massive amount of wood, plus the work of many skilled laborers, and some argued it would interrupt the trout and other fish populations. It wasn't easy to balance with Nature as she shifted and flowed. The river might dry up or begin to flood more often. A hydro-wheel could easily be damaged by a big flood, ruining their investment. I had heard that they were asking for a town vote by next spring, so that work could be finished by next winter if approved.

A pang stabbed me. I might not be here by then—almost certainly, now. So hard to feel part of a community when you might be saying goodbye! *Community the tree; wanderer the woodpecker.* Of course people died and the widowed often remarried, but in general the flow of life was clear by twenty-five. After that, it was the flow of the seasons cycling, the same and yet not the same. At this moment, I was more than ready to give up this transition and fall into something more rhythmic, more reliable.

I'd read histories where people aimed to change every year, to "make progress," as if Life was a straight road and there was some way of winning immortality. I struggled with these old stories that assumed things that they didn't explain, like why it was so important to accumulate possessions like a squirrel hoarded nuts. But the squirrel did it to survive—these people apparently had a community's wealth stored in vast buildings that could house twenty or more, but held a single family.

If these weren't fables, then the ancients seemed to have a hunger sickness, where they couldn't stop gobbling up whatever they touched. I knew there were whole landscapes of broken and discarded things, a researcher's paradise, but when my researcher aunt had told me most of these things were unbroken and still seemed usable, we'd both shaken our heads. It was unfathomable—didn't they live in this same natural world, seeing how plants grew, then bloomed, then died; seeing the leaves come out of the trees, do their job, then die? How had they missed the cycles?

On some level, I realized these wandering thoughts were meant to distract me, and for a short time, it worked. But always, the pain welled up, like a bloody spring, filling me with grief. Who knew that partnering could be so bitter?

The days passed slowly, as if I were pushing into a headwind, forcing myself to complete the daily round. My balance was gone, and I felt guilty walking into shops, pushing myself to be pleasant and proper, knowing I was not living that moment, was drawing energy where I should have given it. For the first time since early childhood, I felt like I wore a mask, that the person I showed wasn't me. I had heard of mask sickness, and knew I should get counseling with an elder, but I hesitated—my mentor position was special, and what if they removed me? So I continued searching for an unnamed something that could release me from my pain and yes, my shame. It wasn't my fault, I argued, and yet I still felt unworthy. The worst was I avoided the library, fearing to run into him when I wasn't prepared. And besides, the words in those old books no longer had the power to draw me in. Words seemed flat and dead compared with this grief. The one benefit was that I felt so much closer to Dale and Su who were also grieving, missing a loved one.

On the Day of Balance, the potlatch was held in the main square. Tables brought from the journeymun's hostel and market booths lined all four sides, with groups and families setting their buffet dishes and potlatch items together, helping me see who was related to whom. The chatting and laughter sounded like the schoolyard in a lower timbre; people were bustling near the stage where the main giveaway would happen, wooden boxes stacked in a small pyramid. I'd found they handled it like my birth town, drawing numbers from a basket, letting people choose in order. The difficult part was matching the gift to the recipient, so why not let a person choose? Some gifts went to the town—donating street lanterns or work time to repair roads.

There weren't many from elsewhere who hadn't married or apprenticed in. I found myself at a table with some wool traders who happened to be in town, a pair of researchers who were digging in a hill nearby, and an acting troupe that would be the day's entertainment. Though I got smiles here and there, my outsider status chafed. I'd been four years in the last town, only a day's walk from my birth town. Now I was a full week's walk away. The customs were different here, with different faces than those myriad cousins who'd made me feel at home. I looked down at my small sketches, walnut ink on some rough unbleached pulp paper, not even the polished sheets used for books. A little grove by the school, the bend in the river to the south of town, a couple of children at play—would anyone want them? They weren't useful, but I hadn't had materials or time to sew up the little pouches that I'd given in the past. Before I could knock myself askew with fretting, I took a deep breath and focused on what was happening around me—this was a ceremony of sharing, and it was the *intent* to share that created community. If only I felt part of it.

I saw Dale frolicking with his younger brother and sister by the water pump—he was pretending to be a horse drinking in the trough. I was relieved to see his playfulness. My gaze flicked from one face to another, fearful of seeing *him* but drinking in the joy and friendliness of others. And sitting under a shade tree, I recognized Beloved Rameda, dressed in an indigo tunic embroidered with pale rose chevrons, receiving the gestures of admiration from a queue of townsfolk. I wondered how it felt to be so old, so revered—to have served the community with such heart that the title "Beloved" was awarded.

The ceremony began with a prayer to the great Mother Gaya, thanking Her for the blessings the community had been given. Then the mayor—a tall, slim woman with slate gray hair—announced the large gifts that were being given to the community by its members. A cart load of wood for community projects, four days of work repairing roads next spring—the gifts had obviously been discussed, with nothing useless being offered.

The smaller gifts began to be chosen by number, and I let my breath out, suddenly realizing I had been holding it. I glanced down at the sketches laid across the table and then determinedly focused on the ceremony—the young mother with her infant walking up to choose a length of fine woolen cloth, Dell skipping forward and choosing a beautifully carved hair clip. Most people seem to have wandered around enough to know what they wanted, so the ceremony wasn't as long as it could have been. To my surprise, several people came right to the sketches and selected one with a smile. I returned their smile gratefully.

A loud, angry voice pierced the ceremony. "All thish fun—thish *giving*—y'all feel so proud of y'selves!" Assed was standing, swaying actually, near the fountain, holding a bottle in one hand and gesturing angrily with the other. Dale and his sisters were huddled near the fountain's bench. "Well, I'm not grateful for the gift you gave to *me*! Ha! You take away my children! You take away my *honor*!" He threw the bottle toward a building; it shattered and everyone gasped.

Then swiftly, before anyone could respond, he turned and grabbed up his youngest, held her tight, and screamed, "She's mine! I made 'er! You have no right t' take my children, my marriage, my life!!"

He began to run, but the crowd finally woke, cut him off, men and women reaching for the girl and trying to grab his arms. Assed was surrounded and it was chaos for several minutes. The green-tunic protection team waded in from the edge of the square, hampered by stunned and frozen townsfolk. Then a woman screamed and Assed howled like a wounded animal. *What had happened??* With the others, I craned to see. The people around him were stepping back, except for two men who held him kneeling on the ground, and a woman who cradled Waali, calling her name softly. It took a minute to realize the child wasn't moving, and at that moment Dara came running up, saw the woman and raced over. She froze and then screamed, "What has been done? Who killed my child!?" Dale and Su ran to her and clung to her knees.

I gasped. Those around me cried out, put their hands to their faces. What *had* happened? A hush as deep as midnight descended on the square. Could she *really* be dead? I watched as the town medic went over, briefly touched Waali, then hugged Dara tightly. Dale reached up toward his sister, but the medic gently turned his hand away. *Oh Dear Mother*—should I go over and comfort him?? I couldn't move. They were escorted toward the health clinic while the protection service got Assed from the ground and walked him toward the Peacekeeper's office.

"My fellow townsmun," the mayor spoke suddenly from the dais. "Due to the tragedy that has just occurred, I would ask us to postpone the rest of today. Those who have not participated will get a chance, but first we must understand and accept this . . . this—" her voice broke, and she struggled to stay calm. "So would those who still have items, please take them back and we will hold the rest of the ceremony on a day to be determined."

"But what has happened?" a voice from the crowd demanded.

"I do not know the whole, but it appears that the child Waali, daughter of Dara and Assed, is dead."

A sigh or groan came from the crowd. People melded into groups, hugging each other and speaking softly. Again I was an outsider, not knowing anyone well enough, feeling I was intruding on their grief. They had known the child for years, I had only known her a mooncycle. Yet I was stunned and it felt like a knife plunged in me. Slowly I returned to my room, exchanged my fancy tunic for my regular one, and lay down.

The pain was overwhelming—like the time I had almost drowned in a swift river. The grief tried to swallow me and I fought it. Surely balance didn't require me to surrender to this?? My heart was straining out of my chest and the tears left hot runnels down my cheeks. I had wept for days when my mother died, but there I had the embrace of my aunts, uncles and cousins. Here I was so alone and some foolish sense of pride, some voice telling me I needed to be "mature," kept me from asking someone else for comfort. I felt I didn't have the right to grieve like this. It didn't make sense, but there it was. All my deep breathing and calling of the spirit to fill me was nothing more than a drop of water on a hot stove. It shouldn't have happened! It was a stupid, stupid accident, wasn't it? Surely the harmony of nature didn't require this sacrifice! I wanted to give up, crawl away home to my family, shut the door and not come out again. I began to panic—how would I face the children tomorrow?? How could I pull myself together? Perhaps I could ask for classes to be suspended, or for the counselors to come and help. Maybe no one would send their children—but I had the responsibility, in case they did.

A sudden rapping at my door made me jump up, nearly knocking over the chair.

"Who's there?"

I was across the room with the doorknob in my hand before I finished speaking. I couldn't bear to see anyone. But it would be so rude, so unheard of, to ignore the knock. I opened the door. Marl stood there with wide eyes, both hands clutching the stems of a half-dozen wildflowers. I froze, then collapsed into his arms in a flood of tears.

He guided me into the room and closed the door, letting my head rest on his shoulder "I don't know what to say to help," he whispered.

"Just be here." I clung tighter and cried until tears were done. Then I pulled away and half blindly scrambled for a handkerchief. "I've slobbered all over you," I apologized.

Tears ran freely down his face as well. "It's okay," he said as we embraced again. And it *was* okay. For the moment our difficulties were forgotten and we just breathed together. I relaxed in the warmth and the beat of his heart. Sorrow wasn't meant to be borne alone. Marl was stroking my back, and I felt a rush of tenderness. I looked up and kissed him lightly, then, as he returned the kiss, more intensely. Within a few minutes, we were on the bed, stroking and pouring kisses on each others' bodies.

‡‡

A few hours later, when we woke from the nap after lovemaking, I felt a surge of guilt—we had turned this tragedy into a sexual encounter! Were we twisted?? But I couldn't resist stroking Marl's chest, kissing it tenderly. Whatever had been the trigger, I was intensely grateful. I looked up, half afraid to see his expression. But I saw nothing besides tenderness; maybe he'd gotten over his fear.

"Thank you, I—" he began, but I put my finger over his lips.

"No need for thanks—I'm as grateful as you are. I felt like we were one person, one heart beating . . ."

"Yes, I see why couples are so mad for each other." He kissed my fingertips. "I want to meet you every night from now on." He giggled; a surprising sound.

I kissed him deeply, then sat up. "I, also . . . I want you. I was connected to you; our souls touch in ways I have never experienced." Afraid I'd gone too far, I added, "I am willing to see how this relationship blooms. We don't have to promise anything; let's enjoy our meetings and watch the growth."

Marl nodded, lying back and closing his eyes. "I'll try not to fear my inner dark. Perhaps this feeling is stronger, after all."

I carried some guilt in my heart about the start of our affair, along with my wild joy. Should I confess to an elder how quickly we had gone from grief to lust? But my daily responsibilities at first kept me from fretting too much. The elders did suspend school for three days, but asked me to assist at the guidance center, helping anyone who came in to get help in regrounding and rebalancing through breathwork. I worked with the children, using breath, art, music and dance, while the elders worked with the parents. This at least was familiar work, and also assuaged my grief. Lil told me that Assed had apparently fought the man who'd tried to take Waali, and in the struggle, the girl's neck had been broken, killing her instantly. Assed would be tried for the killing even though it was partly an accident. Dara had been reunited with her two remaining children, within the Beloved's household, so that they could grieve and adjust to a new life. Even if Assed weren't convicted and branded, he would be exiled. Lil murmured that there was always some chance that Dara would choose to go with him. At my shocked gasp, Lil nodded and said she'd heard of that happening, but the Beloved was working with Dara to accept how dangerous and hurtful to the children it would be.

Walking home that evening, I pondered Lil's words. How could someone *choose* a monster? Then I thought of Marl, of him leaving me so suddenly that day, without a thought to my pain. And yet I let him into my room and my life. I saw Dale attacking the tree sapling, his deep anger more than any child should contain. And yet he was so gentle with his sisters. Now, only one sister—how would *that* loss shape the anger already within him? I shook my head, trying to digest, to put in place these new images. Was this like a canker that attacks the shrub, browning the leaves but not killing the plant? How did nature call forth this ugliness, or was something else at work?

The next half moon cycle was an agonizing struggle between deep joy with Marl and the pain and confusion of watching what seemed like a contagion of ill spirit sweeping through town. Twice in one day, I overheard the beginning of an argument, quickly tamped down but, from the expressions, not ended. And Dell told me that factions were forming, people were going out of their way to avoid certain other people. Lil had mentioned, after inquiring about the children, that they were considering recommending Dara return to her birth town with the children, rather than stay on and be a focus of dissent. The potlatch had been indefinitely postponed, and some were murmuring it might not happen before Solstice. Either another harmony meeting was needed, or something else had to be done. Either way, as an outsider, I could only watch and worry.

But it was on waxing fourth, when I snapped at a clumsy dinner server, that I realized I might be catching it. I apologized immediately, but felt shame through that meal, and took a long walk through town afterward. I turned my gaze from the people, and watched the animals in each yard—the companion dogs who like mentors sat with sprouts and kept them from the street, the rodent-catching cats who lounged on sunlit steps, and the small flocks of chickens fenced near the kitchen gardens.

Once again I noticed how sunlight lifted my heart. The lichen glowing in pale green tuffs on an old cherry, how a shaft of light gave chickens' feathers golden haloes like those sometimes ringing the sun; a rooster's comb such a deep scarlet that it brought a gush of gratitude. So much exquisite beauty—could it be the darkness was something to keep us grounded, because so much beauty could be overpowering? The flock was snapping up the long grass—grass that would not have a chance to seed now . . . so this *was* part of the flow?? I shook my head—*the wise plants do not question the soil.* At least I had found some peace, however fleeting.

That sixth, I was called to the Council office and told that Dara had agreed to leave and her children would be saying goodbye to their classmates the next first.

"I trust you will leave it to Dara to tell the townsfolk," Lil said, "but I ask that you explain to the children, as best you can, that there is no question of running away or failing, but more like being replanted in better soil."

"Yes, of course," I murmured, wondering exactly how one might do that.

In fact, the children were better than some of the adults—Juda telling Su that being with family would help her heal faster, and Lern reminding Dale that he had once complained about not having a brother: "Now you'll have plenty of cousins, who are like brothers." There was little chance of anyone focusing on schoolbooks that day, so when the Beloved had escorted Dale and Su back down the hill, I led the class first in singing, letting them choose the songs, and then outside on a nature walk, identifying and observing how Mother Gaya was bringing the season to a close, pushing plants and insects to hibernate. I marveled at the way the children moved on from their tears, and opened their hearts to the next thing.

I was surprised that evening to get a message asking me to join the small group who would be seeing the family off at dawn the next day, to avoid any large gatherings—at Dara's request. So there was only myself, Rameda, Geralt and Lil on Rameda's front steps as Dara led her children out.

"May the grace of Mother Gaya fill you, heal you and bless you," Lil said as she placed her hands on Dara's shoulders. Dara nodded, quickly turning away, her eyes filling. She was as taut as a bowstring, and the Beloved said nothing, only placed her hands on Dara's shoulders in turn. Geralt patted Dara's back then went to grab her bags and put them on the waiting donkey cart. I had nothing I knew how to say to Dara, so I knelt and whispered *farewell* to each child; I had done my hugging yesterday. As I watched the laden cart lumber away, and Dale twisting on the seat to wave goodbye, I felt my heart clench. My eyes overflowed.

"I hope that this will be the right soil for Dale and his sister to grow," I murmured. "I wish—" I stopped, acutely aware the Beloved stood beside me. The Banfts were already walking up the sidewalk to the Council house.

"I know the councilmun in Dara's birth town; it is a good town, and with cousins, aunts, uncles, Dale and Su will have more support than they could get here. *Not* that you have done poorly. In fact, I would like to talk to you about your work, if you have time to come inside."

I froze. Was I under review? I followed Rameda inside, barely taking note of the soft apricot-toned room, the white pine tables and ancient crystal light catchers that would normally delight me. Rameda gestured toward a stuffed chair, and seated herself on the sofa.

"I may be wrong," Rameda began, "but I sense a burden within you, and I know you have no family here to share that with. Would you be willing to share it with me?"

I felt panic. Would I get help or would I get exiled? I took a deep breath and started. "I fear I may not be . . . capable of the task of mentor. I have become so tense and tight with the children . . ."

"We do not expect our mentor to be a perfect human being. Everyone has become tense recently."

"But I expect more of myself—"

"Which is a good thing, within limits." The Beloved smiled.

I realized I was twirling my hair on a finger; an old childish habit. I lowered my hand to my lap. "All my life I believed we were created for harmony, that it flows in our veins and we simply need to learn the techniques of balance to help when something knocks us askew. Now—now I see darkness in some hearts, darkness that I fear can't be uprooted. And I ask myself is that darkness in *my* heart? Is my vision so askew that I am blind to the real world? It's like the world has a play-acting mask; everything underneath is dark and tangled."

Rameda leaned forward and took my hand with both of her wrinkled soft hands. "In my many years," she began, "I have seen many journeys, some very short but blessed, and some long but filled with pain. The great mystery—the source of this wellspring that creates *us* as well as trees, birds, sky—why this Great Dance sometimes pains, sometimes delights—why we are even alive! That mystery will never be solved on this bank of the Night River. And no one has come back from the other bank to let us know."

"But that—" I feared to contradict. "Those are . . ."

"Just words? Yes." Rameda acknowledged. "But words frame our perceptions. We are a story-making people. There have been many stories about what is on the other bank, if anything—you look surprised? But some do wonder. And some say the stories are there for comfort only. But I have attended many childbeds and deathbeds, and there is a mystery we must grapple with. We can call forth life with our actions and we can cause death with our actions, yet to presume we have the power over life and death is dangerous. Both the calling forth and the ending have consequences far beyond what we understand or can manage."

"I would never presume that," I said. "But I . . . I see now some people might. I don't know how to face people anymore, thinking that within their heart they carry a shadow, like a worm deep in an apple. Could I have done or said something, earlier, that would have stopped—"

"As an outsider?" The Beloved shook her head, leaning back. "Such disorders are like the fevers that too often race through town. Sometimes we have seen and stopped or slowed them. Sometimes they explode in a day or two and take half the town with them. I do blame myself a bit—this unhappy couple was known to us. And yet, suffering is learning, and we cannot stifle growth. 'From the harvest day looking back, the summer seems inevitable.'"

I nodded to acknowledge the old saying then blurted, "I'm afraid I've caught this disorder, this lack of balance. I am as shaky as a small boat on a rushing river. I watch others with suspicion, and jump at the smallest hint of anger. Are people as dark as I think?"

"The way we see others is also part of the story we write for ourselves. I spent part of my younger years trying to see each person as if they were just about to die—it was my attempt to keep the mystery in front of my eyes." The Beloved looked out the window and paused for a long time. "I have to say it caused me great grief, sometimes caused me to act strangely." She chuckled softly. "And in the end

I had to fall back to my everyday point of view. We are not as blind as our animal friends, but we seem to need a certain level of blindness to live in the world."

"But surely the blindness allows this darkness to grow? And where does the darkness come from?? Are people condemned to live these lives of pain or do we have a choice?"

"We have some choices—times when we can choose to stop, assess, and change course; times when we recognize we are acting hatefully even when we feel justified. I have seen many lives where people have struggled, and with great effort have found a different path with more joy. I have also seen times when people have tried mightily and misfortunes just seemed to batter them down. Those times I did wonder who or what caused some people to suffer so much and others to be care-free."

After a long silence, I asked, "Did you ever find a reason?"

Rameda shook her head. "No—it is still part of the mystery. We might as well ask why some plants are stepped on and crushed before they can bloom, or some young animals lose their mothers and thus their lives. There is massive death every day, if you take into account every living thing. We are only part, and our suffering and death may be as random or as destined as the blades of grass."

"But how can you *live*, thinking you could be struck down at any minute?"

"It's true, isn't it? But I understand—didn't I say I had to drop back to my old point of view? Most of us have to live every day blind to the dying and the suffering, unless or until it touches us. We are not that different from the foxes and deer who wander the forest, eating and running from predators." Rameda stood, walked quickly to the other room and came back with a plate of cookies. "Please have some. Dale did not manage to eat all, though he tried hard." She smiled.

I reached for a cookie, though I didn't feel able to eat anything. "Is life that bleak? Yet now it feels like my eyes are open and I'm seeing a different world, a world I'm not sure I want to live in." I struggled to keep my voice level, to speak like an adult.

"Since we do not know the answer to the mystery, each of us creates our own story, each of us *chooses* the meaning that our lives will have in this world. It is a big choice, and I've seen many people who avoid making it, for fear of discovering at the end that it was the wrong story. But *no* story is worse, surely."

"So you say I have to make up my reasons for living?"

"We all do it without thinking. I'm suggesting you can do it with more aware-ness—knowing that this mystery is unsolvable, knowing that our stories could never be proven or disproven, accepting all that and still creating a reason for what you are doing that takes in your best, your dearest hopes and dreams. Acknow-ledging you don't know but having the courage to go forward and bloom, follow-ing your nature and knowing others are following theirs."

"I have not heard this before—when do people learn it?"

"Not everyone does. But you are going to be a mentor, so you need to know." The Beloved winked. "Maybe even a beloved mentor."

I let that sink in. "Were you . . . a mentor?"

"I was. I was graced to be allowed to be part of the early soil that sprouts grew in. I know we speak of the equality of each trade's contribution, but mentorship, I believe, is one of the most sacred."

I felt both honored and anxious. How could I live up?

"But if one's nature, like—for instance—the printer's apprentice Marl, seems to be only sad and fearful? If I saw a child in school like that, should I just allow that nature to be??"

The Beloved looked at me with a shrewd frown, and for a moment I thought I had revealed some fatal flaw. Then she smiled.

"Sometimes the most courageous thing we can do is to refrain from our attempts to make others according to our desires. And the hardest thing we can do is to show others with our example—only that—that they have choices to be aware of. We can show them how *we* choose and how *we* accept consequences. If you saw a daisy, you would not attempt to make it a rose, would you?"

I shook my head.

"It is harder, of course, with children," the Beloved continued. "They seem to be all possibility; one sees greatness and wants it to be so. And we also see those stumbling blocks we fell over and wish to keep the children from falling, too. And we know a child's experience forms the person as surely as soil and weather form the tree."

"In mentor training we were taught it isn't a good idea to get a child to see through adult eyes."

"True. 'Old heads don't fit young shoulders.' And who knows if the lesson learned through a fall or failure is not one of the most important of that life? Thus if we spare them, they may lose a lot more. Yet it's always a risk—and when something goes wrong, it's easy to goad ourselves with guilt. But that really is only the desire to change circumstances." She sighed. "It is only because this town works so hard to ensure the best nurturing that we have such responsible townsfolk. 'As the sapling is trained, so the tree leans.' But none of this is perfect. There will be pain.

"You can be a good mentor," Rameda continued. "You care. But you must not care too much."

Not too much? "I don't understand."

"Does the gardener weep if one cabbage rots? She would go mad. So you must understand—you are the caretaker, not the font of life itself. It is not *you* who bring them in, nor *you* who are the source of their blossoming. You watch, you add nourishment if possible, but you must allow them to be."

"Yesterday, they were actually more capable than some adults." I paused, the thread of an idea forming. It was daring, it was unheard of . . . "And yet, the gardener does make some changes, to help the plants, to make a better garden."

"What do you have in mind?" The Beloved's gaze was on me; I felt my mind was transparent to this shrewd smiling elder.

"I would do nothing, of course, without your approval but I learned something yesterday . . ."

The next seventh was one of the large celebrations, and the town was in the square, facing the stage, waiting for the Beloveds to begin. Many of them reacted in surprise as I wormed my way through the crowd, tapping each student on the shoulder and beckoning them to follow. They filed onto the stage just as Rameda and Lyle came on from the other side and bowed to them. The children bowed back, then arranged themselves to face the crowd.

"We sing to celebrate the grace of the harvest," Lern began, "and in gratitude for each other, sharing and surviving together."

Little Ki stepped forward, and I held my breath. But the ladybug was not awed by the startled adults; she grinned, spread her arms and shouted, "We are the branches of this tree, our town!"

Juda stepped up beside her and continued, "With roots in the soil of ancestors, all of our blood mingling and flowing together. We sing to join our hearts, as our lives are already joined."

Then the children started with a typical autumn hymn, "Join Hands and Praise the Bounty." They stood holding hands, their young voices like a chorus of birds, and I bit back my tears. I noticed I wasn't the only one. At the second verse, some of the townsfolk began to sing along, and soon everyone was singing, holding hands and swaying. Rameda took my hand and squeezed gently. She winked her approval as she sang along.

Possibly it was my imagination, but it seemed like people were more friendly that next week, more impulsively generous, and more laughter broke out on streets and in shops. My heart was lighter, for sure, and when I and Marl met, I felt easier—my heart rested inside, rather than reaching frantically all the time. It would be what it would be. Now I knew I had the Beloved to confide in, and guide me to the next step.

Don't miss Catherine McGuire's new novel, *Lifeline*, now available in print and e-book formats via Founders House Publishing!

Learn more and purchase a copy for yourself at http://www.foundershousepublishing.com/2017/03/lifeline-novel.html

REVIEWS

A STUDY IN LITERARY INFLUENCE

"By the Waters of
   Babylon"
by Stephen Vincent Benét

Originally published 1937
available online

"The Dark Age"
   by Clark Ashton Smith

Originally published 1938

available online at:
http://www.eldritchdark.com/
writings/short-stories/35/the-dark-age

*The Masters of
Solitude*
         by Marvin Kaye
      and Parke Godwin

Avon, 1978

TO MY MIND, ONE OF THE WORST of the mistaken notions circulating in contemporary culture is the belief that it's possible to achieve originality by ignoring everything that's been done in the past. In point of fact, as we've seen over and over again in recent decades, those who do not learn their literary or artistic history are condemned to rehash it, coming up with the same old tropes over and over again under the fond delusion that no one's ever thought of them before. Real originality begins with a good solid grasp of what's already been done; it's when you know what previous creative minds have done in a particular field that you can get a sense of that field's possibilities and pitfalls, and then it becomes a great deal easier to go do something that nobody's done before, and do it well.

This is as true of deindustrial science fiction as it is of any other genre of fiction or, for that matter, any other kind of creative work. There have been some really creative works in the deindustrial genre by people who were starting with a blank sheet of paper and a few hard questions about what happens when industrial civilization takes a long walk off the short dock of its resource base, but there's been much more in the way of rehashed tropes from pop culture—as the editor of the four volumes of the *After Oil* series of deindustrial SF anthologies, trust me, I've seen 'em all. Far more often than not, the writers who produce reliably good deindustrial science fiction have read other works in the genre, thought about them, and come up with their own personal responses to the challenges of the future ahead of us.

Now and then, in fact, it's possible to watch ideas from certain early works in the field weaving their way through later works. The novel that stands at the center of this issue's column, Marvin Kaye and Parke Godwin's frankly brilliant *The Masters of Solitude*, is a

fine example of the species. Kaye and Godwin, when they started work on their novel, knew their way through the deindustrial genre, and they drew a significant part of their inspiration from two forgotten classics of the genre, both of which were published almost exactly forty years previously: Stephen Vincent Benét's "By the Waters of Babylon" and Clark Ashton Smith's "The Dark Age."

Stephen Vincent Benét doesn't normally find his way into lists of classic science fiction writers, deindustrial or otherwise. His book-length narrative poem about the Civil War, *John Brown's Body*, was widely hailed in its day, and a couple of centuries from now will probably be considered one of the great works of twentieth-century English verse; most of his other works were conventional literary fiction and verse. His one serious venture into science fiction, though, was a corker. "By the Waters of Babylon" was one of the first serious attempts in fiction to imagine what North America would look like after the modern world was a distant memory, and it had an immense influence on later explorations of the same territory.

It's also, by the way, a great story. A first person narrative, it's told by John, who is a priest and the son of a priest, and so has the right to go into the Dead Places to salvage metal —those readers who know their way around my deindustrial novel *Star's Reach* now know another of the sources of my invented profession of "ruinman." He is one of the Hill People, a tribal folk who still recall the trick of literacy and have retained such basic technologies as the spinning wheel. John has long dreamed of traveling east eight suns' journey to the Place of the Gods, which it is forbidden to look upon. When he comes of age, his father tests his vision with the omen sticks, and when the omens are favorable, gives John his blessing and sends him off to follow his strong dream.

He passes through the forest and comes to the mighty river called Ou-dis-son, the Sacred, the Long. (We pronounce that "Hudson" these days.) From its banks, visible in the distance to the south is the Place of the Gods, with its vast ruined buildings stained red in the sunset light. Despite the taboos of his tribe, despite his fear that gods or demons will see him there and eat him up, John knows he must cross the river to the Place of the Gods. Half terrified and half exultant, he builds a raft, paints himself for death, and sings his death-song as he poles himself out into the current and crosses the river.

I'll leave what he discovers in the Place of the Gods for readers to find for themselves; "By the Waters of Babylon" is readily come by online or off, and any aficionado of deindustrial fiction owes it to himself or herself to chase down a copy and read it. If parts of it seem almost clichéd now, that's because so many of its basic ideas became omnipresent in later fiction; when it first appeared, it must have shaken many of its

readers to the core by its sheer unexpectedness.

The same can be said of the second story I want to discuss here, Clark Ashton Smith's "The Dark Age." A contemporary of Benét's, Smith was on the other end of the literary spectrum of the age: while Benét wrote for high-end magazines and literary journals, Smith wrote for the pulp magazines, which sold to an audience composed mostly of teenage boys for ten cents a copy. The irony—and it's a familiar one in literary history—is that it's Smith and his fellow pulp authors such as H.P. Lovecraft, not Benét and his peers, that most people think of today when they recall the imaginative fiction of the Jazz Age.

Smith made his reputation with glittering fantasy tales that combined gorgeous prose with a wry sense of humor and plots that, as often as not, ended with the protagonist meeting a gruesome fate. "The Dark Age" is thus very nearly as much of an outlier for Smith as "By the Waters of Babylon" was for Benét: a spare, bleak, thoughtful tale that is as far as I know the first attempt in fiction to talk about the possibility of preserving science in an isolated quasi-monastic retreat while the rest of the world crashes into barbarism around it.

The retreat in Smith's story is a laboratory in the mountains, built like a fortress and guarded by defensive shields powered by solar energy. A handful of scientists barricaded themselves within it while war, famine, and epidemic depopulated the vast urban centers far away, and they and their descendants remained there while the scattered survivors of the collapse regressed to Stone Age conditions.

Only once did one of the Custodians, as the scientists called themselves, leave the safety of the fortified laboratory. He called himself Atullos, befriended the local barbarian tribe, married one of their women, and had a son. He taught the tribe to mine ore and smelt metals, and had grander plans, but died on a solitary journey leaving his son, Torquane, who had scarcely learned the alphabet and the rudiments of arithmetic. Like John, the priest's son in Benét's tale, Torquane nurtured the dream of seeking out the forbidden place, and like John, he eventually set out on that journey. What he found there, again, I'll leave to readers to discover for themselves; "The Dark Age" is a capable tale by a masterly wordsmith and, like "By the Waters of Babylon," deserves to be read by fans of deindustrial fiction.

In fact, both these stories *were* read, repeatedly, by later authors in the genre, and that's where the benefits of knowing the history of a genre become luminously visible. Quite a few of the post-nuclear holocaust novels of the 1950s and 1960s—a thriving genre at the time, for obvious reasons—have Benét's and Smith's fingerprints all over them, in the form of images, incidents, and ideas that came straight out of one of the two stories just discussed. In some cases those were simply recycled in more or less intact

form—one of the fixtures of my misspent youth, André Norton's lively postapocalyptic tale *Star Man's Son*, centered on the adventures of a young man from a scientific enclave like that of the Custodians poling his way through ancient ruins on a raft like the one John the priest's son used on his journey to the Place of the Gods. In some cases, though, familiar borrowings like these were transmuted into something richer and stranger—and that's part of the process that gave rise to Marvin Kaye and Parke Godwin's *The Masters of Solitude.*

Science fiction, deindustrial and otherwise, had matured considerably by the time Kaye and Godwin got to work, and it shows. Their tale has a richly imagined historical and geographical setting of a sort that next to nobody was putting in their fiction in the 1930s. It takes place in what's now the northeastern United States some two thousand years from now, when modern industrial civilization is a distant memory. One of the striking features of the setting is that there's no apocalyptic downfall in the past, just ordinary history: an invasion from the west by another people, the Jings, who left their name and some of their genetics behind before fading from memory in turn.

Most of the countryside belongs to the covens, rural clans with a culture and religion descended from modern Wicca. In the mountains to the west are the Kriss, who worship a dead god. The other way, running along the seacoast in the old urban belt from

Washington D.C. to New York City and beyond, is the City: an urban enclave maintaining the high technologies and scientific culture of an earlier day, its people prolonging their lives for centuries by advanced biomedicine, their society sheltered from the surrounding tribal world by an electronic barrier that shreds minds. For many centuries there has been no contact between the City and the rest of its world—until a City dweller, Judith Singer, walks out through the barriers in search of a legendary weapon of the ancient world.

She doesn't find it, but like Atullos in Smith's story, she marries and has a son. Her husband is Garick, of the Shando coven—we pronounce that "Shenandoah" these days—who starts out as a big dumb apple farmer's son and grows through the arc of a long and troubled life into a great and tragic figure. Her son is named Singer; after his mother dies, he inherits her knowledge and her quest for the legendary weapon—and Singer has a half-brother Arin, Garick's son by the Shando priestess Jenna, whose destiny is entwined with his.

For the covens face the return of a familiar horror: bubonic plague, descending again from the north as it has so many times in the past. Garick, who is now master of the Shando coven, sets out to unite the covens and the Kriss into a single force powerful enough to pressure the City, through war if it comes to that, to open its doors, share its knowledge, and help turn aside the pandemic. Yet the Kriss are playing a cold game of their own—and in the three-handed poker game that follows, played for the highest stakes, the covens, the Kriss, and the City will all be changed forever.

It's a bravura performance, and among the things that make it so impressive are a cascade of little homages to the stories by Benét and Smith already discussed. Many of these are details, turns of phrase or incident that recall this or that detail in the adventures of John the priest's son or Torquane; some of them are major plot points important enough that even hinting at them here would give away too much of a well-plotted tale; not one of them is out of place in the story, but their effect on the literate reader is like that of the little half-seen faces that peer out of the intricate carvings of medieval cathedrals, winking a silent acknowledgment at the viewer: yes, you've noticed me.

More broadly, though, one of the things that makes *The Masters of Solitude* a major work of deindustrial SF is precisely that its authors have read, reread, and reflected on some of the earlier classic works in that field, and then gone beyond them. Stephen Vincent Benét pioneered the story of the venturesome young man from a tribal deindustrial society making the long and perilous journey to the forbidden city of the ancients; Clark Ashton Smith pioneered the tale of the enclave of scientists and its problematic relationships with the surrounding tribal cultures. Kaye and Godwin took both of these themes, picked them up where Benét and Smith left them, and wove them into a powerful tale of love, loss, disillusionment, and the ending of an age.

The tale is worth reading, but the example is also worth following—and one of the points behind this column's disinterment of forgotten and half-forgotten tales is precisely the hope that today's and tomorrow's authors in the genre will learn from Kaye and Godwin the way they learned from Benét and Smith, and go on to create their own splendid and moving tales of the deindustrial future.

In future issues of *Into the Ruins*, I plan on continuing this column and surveying the desolate but enticing landscapes portrayed by past authors of deindustrial SF. While I have a good many books already lined up to review, there's doubtless no shortage of stories of that kind that I haven't read or don't remember. If you have favorites you'd like to propose for review, or for that matter really dreadful examples of the species, by all means drop me a note c/o *Into the Ruins* at joel@intotheruins.com, or by mail at:

Figuration Press
3515 SE Clinton Street
Portland, OR 97202

Many thanks!

New York 2140
by Kim Stanley Robinson

Orbit, 2017

THE BEST WRITERS NOT ONLY bring their readers new ways of envisioning the world, but new vocabularies for talking about the world. Sometimes the neologisms and words they coin break out and become part of the larger culture. Robert Heinlein gave us the word *grok* and aging hippies still bandy it about at outdoor music festivals to show how deeply they understand one another. George Orwell's term *newspeak* about the propagandistic use of language by Big Brother is now a subject for newspaper op-ed pieces as pundits grapple with the current administration. As I sit down to write this, after a long work week spent in front of the computer, the word *repaleolithization* comes to mind. It's from Kim Stanley Robinson's earlier book on climate change, *Fifty Degrees Below*. It is something I could have used a bit of today as it refers to a lifestyle shift used to reestablish sanity for the human body and mind, and consists mainly of activities mostly abandoned by the urban denizens of late industrial capitalism. As I sit here typing I think about how nice it will be to take some time off soon, and walk out on the land with family and friends, talking and cooking under the stars, staring at a fire instead of a screen. These are some of the things repaleolithization consists of. Kim says it can be thought of as a form of "landscape restoration for the brain," and the landscape, both inner and outer, is something he returns to again and again throughout the arc of his novels, of which *New York 2140* is his eighteenth.

The way humans interact with the landscape is a recurring theme across his work. Sometimes it is through terraforming, sometimes via artwork. In his epic *Mars* trilogy on the colonization of the red planet, massive geoengineering projects are used to transform it into a place hospitable to life. In his novel *2312* the main character is a landscape artist after the manner of Andy Goldsworthy. In *Shaman*, his novel of the Ice Age, the hero of the story is a cave painter, and readers catch a glimpse of some of the forces that may have been at work behind the earliest drawings of animal images on the granite walls of Lascaux. While the main thrust of *New York 2140* is on economics, Robinson continues to riff on themes of human interaction and collaboration with the landscape, showing how the two are inextricably joined in ecological feedback loops. Kim has been hanging around the anthropocene for awhile and in his new book he gives readers a distillation of the human economy's effect on global ecology, and the intimate connections between the two.

Throughout the book Robinson throws in little nuggets about the historical geography of New York City —how it was built around an estuary, on swamps and bogs, and on the banks of rivers and bays. The whole project of such a vast and diverse city evolving from small encampments and villages to the huge skyscraper sprawl it has become can be considered a terraforming project in itself. Yet eventually mother nature bites back at this built environment. In the backstory of the book, two major events in the trajectory of climate change have caused a drastic rise in sea level that spills over into social and economic turmoil. Kim calls these events the Pulses, when the ocean rose up to reclaim what had once been her own, devastating coastal cities. In the New York of 2140, whole boroughs are drowned. The roofs of Queens and the Bronx have become new reefs. Some people squat in the upper floors of buildings, those parts of a house that sit above the high tide line. Every now and then a building will fall over into the water. These neighborhoods are part of what has come to be called the intertidal and are now subject to market speculation and the blooming of a new real estate bubble.

Other parts of the city have fared better, though still affected by the water. The streets of New York are gone. They have been replaced by canals and traffic is either by boat, or through sky walk tubes connecting one building to another. Manhattan is the borough where most of the book takes place, and the story is tied to the fate of the MetLife tower, now a vast retrofitted housing cooperative. The kaleidoscopic, intertextual narratives are told from the vantage point of multiple protagonists, all living in the Met, packed in like sardines, getting on remarkably well despite the closeness.

Vlade is the superintendent of the Met, charged with protecting it and the people who live there. He has a thousand details on his plate to be mindful of. When two computer programmers in the finance sector go missing and unknown assailants attempt to sabotage the building, Vlade must tighten his belt to keep things in order, managing the dock and keeping an eye on leaks and the integrity of the entire structure. Two "water rat" orphan boys who have adopted the Met as their base give Vlade something else to worry about as they continue to get into trouble searching for treasure in the ruins of the city with a makeshift diving bell. These boys help bridge the gap between Vlade and his estranged wife Idelba, who is the captain of a massive boat stationed out on the waters where Coney Island used to be, her crew engaged in the long-term project of dredging sand up from the bottom and dumping it further in to create a new beach.

Amelia Black is a cloud celebrity whose show *Assisted Migration* is watched by millions. When in town, she keeps her dirigible airship tied to the mast on top of the Met. Amelia engages in a form of rewilding, reintroducing species to various habitats and corridors, moving endangered species out of collapsing ecosystems to locations where they might have a chance at survival. In 2140 only about four hundred polar bears remain in the wilds of the arctic, and their numbers continue to dwindle. The bears get landlocked in Greenland in the spring when the sea ice thaws, keeping them from hunting their oceanic food supply of seals. Amelia gets the bright idea of transporting the bears down south. Way down south to Antarctica. There they will have enough open space to regrow their numbers and the seal population is still strong enough for them to eat. One thing Amelia doesn't count on is opposition from radical environmentalists who think of Antarctica as the last pure landscape on earth and that transplanting animals there is a form of desecration.

Placed in intervals throughout the book is a long essay on economics and ecology attributed to an anonymous citizen. For readers who are strictly interested in the overlapping narratives of the many character—who also include a housing lawyer, an old man with a massive map collection, a hedge fund trader, a police inspector, and two hackers—the essays can be skipped without loss to the story. I enjoyed them even if I was sometimes eager to get back to the main action. Science fiction is a literature of ideas and using this format gives Kim the opportunity to present his informed speculation about potential political economies in a time when all the great coastal cities of the world will be a lot wetter than they already are. He uses them to fill in the timeline of history between now and 2140 with a strong fermented brew of materials science, aquaculture, food systems, new social experiments, and creativity born from coping with destruction. But we don't need to wait until then to get started. The dizzying presentation of myriad ideas are worth tinkering with and implementing now. My head is still spinning in a most delightful way from the read. And after a bit of time reacquainting myself with the elements outside, I'm going to look through the book again to see what else can be reaped from it in preparation for the high tides of the future.

— *Justin Patrick Moore*
sothismedias.com

Don't miss a single issue of Into the Ruins

Subscribe Today

Visit intotheruins.com/subscribe
or send a check for $39 made out to Figuration Press to:

Figuration Press
3515 SE Clinton Street
Portland, OR 97202

Don't forget to include the name and address of where you want your subscription sent, as well as which issue you would like to start with.

Already a subscriber? Your subscription may be expiring!

Renew Today

Visit intotheruins.com/renew
or send a check for $39 made out to Figuration Press to
the address above

Don't forget to include the name and address attached to your current subscription and to note that your check is for a renewal. Your subscription will be extended for four more issues.

Thank you for reading!

Printed in Great Britain
by Amazon